Stephen H. Tyng

Forty Years' Experience in Sunday-Schools

Stephen H. Tyng

Forty Years' Experience in Sunday-Schools

ISBN/EAN: 9783337272364

Printed in Europe, USA, Canada, Australia, Japan

Cover: Foto ©Andreas Hilbeck / pixelio.de

More available books at **www.hansebooks.com**

FORTY YEARS'

Experience in Sunday-Schools.

BY

STEPHEN H. TYNG, D.D.,

RECTOR OF ST. GEORGE'S CHURCH, NEW YORK.

NEW YORK:

SHELDON & COMPANY.

BOSTON: GOULD & LINCOLN.

1860.

STEREOTYPED BY
SMITH & McDOUGAL,
82 & 84 Beekman-st., N. Y.

PRINTED BY
PUDNEY & RUSSELL,
79 John-street, N. Y.

INTRODUCTION.

THE importance of the subject of this little volume none can doubt. There is a familiarity in treating it, and a desultory method pursued in its discussion which may be considered inappropriate for a book. I have only to say, the chapters herein contained, were so many distinct letters addressed to a friend who was the Superintendent of a Sunday-school, at his own request. After a publication in the INDEPENDENT had given them a very extensive circulation, their compact publication in the present form was also solicited. They are the simple language of personal experience and observation in the field of which they treat. They may be the instrument of suggesting other and better thoughts and experience to other minds. I can not but hope they will be made useful to many. If they shall but set Christians and ministers to thinking, inquiring, and speaking, even in opposition to some of the sentiments they contain, they will do good. There can be but one result to which conscientious thought and inquiry must lead, and with that the end and purpose of the book will be so far attained. To his brethren in the ministry of the whole Church of our Lord Jesus Christ, and to his sympathizing friends, the Sunday-school teachers in all the Churches, the author gratefully presents his little work, praying for their countenance, and the Lord's blessing.

St. George's Rectory.
New York, August 1, 1860.

CONTENTS.

I.

MY DEAR FRIEND : You ask for some notes of my personal experience in connection with Sunday-schools, and some of the results of that experience. I shall be glad to gratify you in a very simple and desultory way, having no time to arrange any thing in a more methodical or didactic shape. The proposal will lead me first to a few reminiscences of my own connection with these interesting nurseries of the Church of Christ.

In the year 1819, when a candidate for the ministry, I was first sent forth by Bishop Griswold, as a young laborer in the Gospel, under the title of what we call in the Episcopal Church a Lay Reader, which included, in those days, the utmost range of personal exhortation and preaching. I was directed by him to the temporary charge of a small, vacant Episcopal church in Quincy, Mass. A few scattered families and individuals made up the congregation, of whom two ladies, still living and useful in the church, agreed to unite with me in the opening of a Sunday-school. Such an enterprise had never been undertaken or seen by either of us ; nor had there ever been a Sunday-school in the town. But the zeal and love of young Christians, earnest in the Lord's service, will furnish both the model and the accomplishment of what they are prompted to undertake for him. We scoured the town among the families to whom we had access, and among whom we could circulate our notices, to invite children of all kinds to our school on the appointed Sabbath. To our amazement, when the morning arrived, we found perhaps fifty children assembled, a larger number than our whole congregation had ever been before. Our youthful hearts rejoiced, and our inexperienced hands were full. There were four teachers besides myself—the two young ladies, and two young men whose family attended the church. We knew but little of the work we had undertaken, but we had hearts that desired to work, and a love for the enterprise with which the Lord had so remarkably honored us. We labored on with a happy spirit and successful results. The first boy whose name I took at the opening of that school, has been for more than twenty years a distinguished minister of the Episcopal Church. One of the two male teachers gave his life to the Foreign Missionary work, and died in Ceylon. The other was taken away while in his course of theological study, and the two ladies are still living, active and useful in the Lord's work.

Little as I knew then, this first Sunday-school was a very exciting and stirring event of my life. It had the effect of an entire enlistment of my affections and efforts in this work. But my subsequent early ministry was for several years in a very scattered and wide-spread country, where the gathering of large Sunday-schools was impossible. And yet I have but the last week received a letter from the Sunday

school missionary laboring in that region of the
South, informing me that thirty public primary school-rooms in the county are now offered
for Sunday-school occupation, and asking my
co-operation in furnishing means for libraries
for their use. So remarkably has the work
progressed and enlarged in our day.

In the spring of 1829, I was called to St.
Paul's church, in the city of Philadelphia,
where there had been Sunday-schools, very complete and well arranged, from 1816. There
were in those schools perhaps four hundred
children. They made a very effective arrangement in both sexes, from adult Bible-classes
down to infant schools. The best and most
intelligent members of the church were engaged in them. Many of the most influential
of the officers of the church were also occupied in them. They were wisely, intelligently,
and efficiently conducted. They made the very
field of labor for which I had longed, and which
I ardently and instantly embraced. I organized
a weekly lecture on the lesson for the teachers,
and had beside a weekly Bible-class of ladies,

including the female teachers. I spent every
Sabbath morning in a personal visitation of all
the schools, examining the classes and aiding to
the utmost of my power in the work of teaching, often having the opportunity to take some
vacant class, and thus come into direct contact
with the children themselves. I gave every
Sunday afternoon, when our public service was
in the evening, to a personal address to all the
schools combined.

A whole generation has since passed away.
The children of that day are now the active
mature workers in our churches. More than
ten of them have become preachers of the
Gospel. Over one hundred and fifty have
given themselves to the Lord's service in the
lay fellowship and labor of the churches.
How many more of all these clusters of
fruit have been gathered since, from the same
heavenly plant, I have no adequate means
of knowing. Those schools have all been
maintained in all their efficiency to the present
time. Never were they so strong and prosperous as under the present rector of St. Paul's,

who was one of the boys of that day, and who has proved himself so earnest, and successful in the Sunday-school work, in his ministry since. I imagine these schools may be regarded as a model of successful effort at the present day.

Five years' ministry at St. Paul's prepared me with a knowledge and experience which were brought into operation in the successful founding and establishment of the Church of the Epiphany in the same city. That church was founded upon the Sunday-school. Its energy and strength were given to the school. Previously the Sunday-school had been considered an appendage to the church, and by some ministers and members a troublesome appendage. We founded this church with the distinct understanding and plan, that the Sunday-school should be the main and prominent object of regard, and its convenience and successful operation thoroughly provided for; and we carried out this principle completely. These schools in their general features were arranged as those at St. Paul's. They were opened in December, 1834, with four teachers and ten scholars in the male school, and five teachers and fifteen scholars in the female school. They were left by me in 1845, when I removed to New York, with thirty-eight teachers and three hundred and eighty-one scholars in the male, and forty-two teachers and four hundred and twenty-three scholars in the female department. I have never seen elsewhere, schools at all equal to them in the whole scheme and elements of successful operation. They were blessed with many very precious evidences of the Lord's presence and grace, and large numbers from them were gathered to the table of the Lord, and already many young ministers are in the Lord's work, who have gone forth from them. To these schools, I continued my habit of a weekly lecture to teachers, a weekly female Bible-class, a monthly address to the schools, and the giving of every Sunday morning to a supervision of the work as it went on. In these I established also an Anniversary, with the donation of books to every scholar, as a token of our mutual interest and affection. And when I survey my

2

Philadelphia work of sixteen years, no part of it seems to me to have been so remunerative and happy as my connection with my Sunday-schools. Incidents and facts of this connection may come up in some future communications. But they were happy, useful, and improving hours which were so occupied. And God was pleased very largely to add his blessing to the work. No toil could be more delightful, or bearing richer fruits.

II.

ERHAPS an apology is necessary for entering so largely upon the history of my own personal relations to Sunday-schools. But understanding your desire to be a practical account of my individual experience and observation of the working and results of these precious nurseries of our youth, I saw no way to get at it so simply and naturally, as by the introduction of a personal narrative. Do not blame me then in the utterance of stories of personal affection and interest. In 1845, I was most unexpectedly transferred in my ministry to this city. St. George's church had always been distinguished for a lively and active interest in Sunday-schools, and honored by the labors of a faithful pastor and an earnest body of teachers.

But our removal of the church to a new field of labor occurred so soon after my coming into the pastoral relation here, that I had no opportunity in the old church to do more than to co-operate, as earnestly and actively as I could, in the limited schools which I found in Beekman street. We entered upon our new undertaking in the autumn of 1847, but did not occupy our new church until November, 1848, nor till a year after that, had we any building apart from the church in which the schools might be held. Till then we struggled on in the gallery of the church, in a very scattered and unsatisfactory way.

But our new enterprise was in its very foundation and purpose, like the Epiphany, a Sunday-school church. Several of the officers of the church became engaged in the work. The Vestry adopted it and provided for it in the most liberal and effective manner. Appropriations and arrangements for its convenience and accommodation were made with cheerfulness and pleasure. A cordial and lively interest in the work always marked their deliberations and plans ; and much of the prosperity of these schools has depended upon this zeal and generous interest in them on the part of the Vestry of this church. We have never needed funds, or laborers, or affectionate support, which have not been at once forthcoming and efficient. The children of our congregation have, as a rule, uniformly attended our Sunday-school, and thus every **family** in the church, rich and poor, have felt themselves possessed of a common property and a common responsibility in everything which has concerned the welfare and success of the undertaking.

We commenced our school in October, 1847, in the University chapel, with about thirty children of all classes, and in the year of our occupation there, could grow but little. But it was a living coal, however small, and though a little matter, kindled for us a great fire. In the spring of 1850, when we held our first anniversary, we had grown to forty-two teachers and five hundred and five scholars. This was the first year of our meeting in our new chapel, and the first spring after the completion of our

2*

church. In two more years, so rapidly had we grown, that our third anniversary gave us a total of one thousand and two. Our infant school, which was commenced in the organ gallery of the church with eleven children in 1849, had now enlarged to two hundred and eighty-eight, under the same teacher. The crowds in our one building, and the multitudes of poor children still seeking admission, compelled us after this to engage in the establishment of a mission school, of which I shall desire to speak in a separate account. Our sixth anniversary, the first which included the mission school, presented ninety-five teachers and one thousand five hundred and thirty-six scholars. And this has remained about our average number since. Our tenth anniversary, in the spring of 1859, closed with one hundred and six teachers and one thousand five hundred and sixty-five scholars. But in these ten years more than ten different schools had been established by other churches in the field which we had at first occupied alone. I had always anticipated a diminution of our numbers as inevitable, un-

der a process like this. We have found, however, no essential difference in our own number,
while there are probably near two thousand
children now gathered in other Sunday-schools
of various kinds, within the limits which were
then our sole domain. It is to me a very
happy and grateful thought that our efforts
have not been without their influence in encouraging and fostering these adjuvant efforts,
so that God may have made us a blessing beyond our own direct labor and immediate relations. With the attainment of such a result,
I should have felt no surprise, and I trust no
sorrow, at a necessary lessening of our numbers, in the more general spreading of the influence and the work around us. If our poor
children may be taught the Saviour's word, and
fed with the Saviour's love, I trust it will be
always our part and purpose only to rejoice,
whoever may be made the blessed instruments
of the glorious result.

In the organization of the schools now under my more immediate notice and care, ex-
cepting for the present all reference to our mis-

sion schools, we have six different rooms for
instruction. One infant school under two
teachers, of three hundred and twenty children ; another infant school under one teacher,
of one hundred and thirty-five children ; two
female Bible-classes, one of fifty-seven and another of thirty-nine young ladies, in two separate rooms, under two female teachers ; a
young men's Bible-class of thirty-three members, with one teacher ; and in our main
school, two hundred and seventy-eight girls
and two hundred and forty boys, under fifty-
eight teachers. All these have always been
under the superintendence of one executive
head as superintendent. We have thus means
and arrangements for appropriate teaching for
every age and class from three years old to full
maturity. All these departments are in complete and successful operation, and under the
most harmonious arrangement and control.
For the first seven years of our growth and
establishment here, I was favored with the
aid of two valued and efficient laymen, who
successively had the superintendence of this

large array of youth. Since their necessary separation from the work, I have taken the entire personal superintendence myself. From the commencement of this school, I have never failed to go through all these rooms and classes, and to maintain a personal inspection and oversight of the whole operation in all its branches and its practical details. For the last three years I have given my whole time and presence to their actual personal management, during the whole period of the session. If you should be disposed to ask why I have undertaken this additional labor, I can only say, because my whole experience of the operation has so enlarged my sense of its importance, and my affectionate personal interest therein, that I have felt it a vast pleasure and enjoyment to be myself personally and constantly engaged in its duties and its success. I have around me valued laymen whom I should be glad to see earnestly at work, and very faithful teachers who are constantly so. But thus far, neither the amount of actual toil, nor the importance of keeping the lay power of the

church engaged, has been sufficient to overcome my own selfish delight in the occupation,
or my unwillingness to relinquish it. Perhaps
in this I have been wrong. But I have seen
some very blessed and valuable results arising
from the labors thus pursued. And in a future
consideration of some general elements and
principles involved and developed in the whole
process, I shall have occasion to speak of this
subject more particularly again.

In these schools, from their commencement,
I have given a weekly lecture on every Friday
evening, on the lesson for the ensuing Sunday,
trying in this method to illustrate not merely
the subjects involved, but also the simplest and
most effectual manner of teaching. The great
object in this lecture always is to bring out the
important evangelical principles which are exhibited in every portion of Scripture history
as well as teaching, that our children may
learn to see the Saviour, and something of his
grace, everywhere in the words of Divine inspiration. I have always thought that every
portion of the Word of God speaks of his sal-

vation, in some illustration or description, either of its agencies, its principles, or its results. And therefore if teachers can be assisted in bringing out this hidden light of Divine truth, that it may all shine upon the Saviour, to their children, as it all shines from him in the Word, they may gain advantages of precious value to themselves while they are imparting like precious instruction in living truths to the children before them. I have thrown this into the shape of a familiar personal lecture, rather than a catechetical examination with the teachers, because the interest seems greater to them, and the same opportunity is given to other members of the congregation who desire it, to gain the same benefit of simple practical instruction in the Word of God.

I have always felt the importance of some further personal relations to the Sunday-school than could be maintained merely through the teachers. And from the time of my first removal to Philadelphia, I established a monthly sermon for the children, in order to bring my

personal instructions more directly to bear
upon them.   This monthly address on Sunday
afternoon I have continued until the past year,
when my morning opportunity seemed to render it no longer especially necessary.   But
when our new St. George's was opened in
1848, such was the attendance of youth around
me, that I was not satisfied with the amount
of direct attention which was given to them.
I then made the sermon of every Sunday afternoon a sermon to the young.   This plan I
have continued to the present time.   It has
been one of the most interesting and effective
of my labors in the ministry.   I have pursued
a course of connected instruction in series of
plain and intelligible lectures on various Scripture biographies, of which Ruth and Esther
have been published,—on Scriptural plants,
and animals, and mountains,—on Scriptural
religion as exhibited in youth,—on the Para-
bles, etc., till I have now gone through eleven
years of such continued instruction.   And the
Lord has been pleased very graciously and
mercifully to own this teaching in many

cases of conversion to himself, and in much
real edification of youth in his service. I
have considered no part of my work more
valuable and important than this. And certainly no portion of it has seemed so .popu-
lar and acceptable to others. In addition
to these instruments, I have employed lectures
and exhibitions with the magic lantern as an
instrument of interesting the children in the
school, and creating a happy and innocent op-
tunity of amusement for them. Other elements of our plan will occur for notice in
some future heads of remark upon this subject.
Thus fifteen more years of my personal relations to Sunday-schools have passed away,
and another generation has come to maturity
under my care. And I still look upon the occupation with increasing delight. It seems to
me every year more and more remunerative
and encouraging as a ministry for Christ, in
every way within my power to feed his lambs.

3

III.

FAILURE OF TEACHERS.—ADVANTAGES OF SUNDAY-SCHOOLS.—
CONVERSION OF CHILDREN.—RESULTS OF EFFORTS.—RE-
VIVAL IN ST. PAUL'S.—FRUITS OF TEACHING.

MY outline of personal history has brought me to a point at which, perhaps, I may be permitted to apply the results of experience and observation to a wider and more abstract field, in reference to the important subject involved. Forty years' active interest and intelligent consideration connected with our Sunday-schools, have convinced me more and more of their value and efficiency as an instrument of blessing to the church of God. During this period I have seen the waxing and waning of many individual agencies in this connection. I have known brethren who were once earnest advocates of the system, and have preached and prayed for its prosperity, giving up in despair

or in disgust, and refusing longer to bear the
anxiety and trial involved in its support. I
have seen many teachers, of both sexes, wearied
and exhausted, either with the fatigue of the
labor, or the failure of success, and retiring
from the whole field, to undertake its cultivation no more. I can only say for myself,
the influence of the operation on my mind has
been precisely the reverse. 'Never have I felt
the importance of the work more really ; and
never was I more determined to continue my
labors in it while my Master shall give me
opportunity and his blessing. And I have, in
the circle of my most valued acquaintance,
many teachers who have labored faithfully for
years, and are still unwearied, and some who
were active in the work before I began, and are
still earnestly engaged therein. I desire to record my testimony as the result of my whole
experience, that, in my judgment, there is no
department of Christian labor more vitally
influential upon the triumphs of the Gospel—
more remunerative in its immediate results of
blessing to the soul engaged—more effective in

maintaining and enlarging the best interests of the Christian church and the most efficient operation of the Christian ministry.

Yet my personal experience has not been without a clear perception of the difficulties and defects in the practical operation, and in the way of full and desired success. But these lead to the consideration of the very practical question, *What advantages have we a right to expect from our Sunday-schools, as fair and legitimate results?* This is a question which long practice, and, perhaps, still more, repeated disappointments, will very naturally force upon the mind. And the more earnest is the interest felt in the operation, necessarily the more anxious and habitual will be the consideration of this question. My own answer to this question, arising from anticipations always cherished, and from actual results partly attained, would involve several important particulars.

I should, first of all, say, we have a right to expect the actual conversion of our children, under the influence of Divine truth faithfully

and simply taught. The grand uniform instruction of the Sunday-school is to be in the
Word of truth ; and supposing the praying
and experienced Christian teacher expounding
and applying this, with a dependence on the
heavenly teaching to bless his own, we surely
may look for that manifestation of the power
of this transforming truth to the children's
minds and hearts. This, or any subsequent
suggestion will not be pursued by me, in any
shape of controversy or argument. I shall
simply state what are my own personal views
and conclusions. I cannot consent to any
lower result, as a satisfactory object and purpose in a teacher's mind, than this. The
teacher's thought and plan must be that of a
real and living messenger of Christ, to a little
congregation whose eternity may depend upon
this immediate relation and opportunity, and
whose salvation, never to be secured but in a
cordial acceptance of a Saviour's finished work
of love, may be secured under the present
agency, and with the Divine blessing on the
means now faithfully employed. And in the

13*

faithful and earnest employment of these means we have a right to look for the conversion of children to Jesus, and their living by the Holy Spirit for God. The qualifications of adequate teachers I do not now consider, but suppose them fully and actually possessed and exercised. This being so, the pastor, the parents, and the church may justly desire and expect that God will bless the work with this all-important result. A seed will be growing up in the church who shall really serve him.

When I survey the actual results of blessing which I have witnessed under this one great head, I have much reason to bear my testimony that God has never failed to bless his Word, thus faithfully ministered, in some degree. I certainly have never seen the fullness of these spiritual fruits which I have desired. Yet I have not been without frequent proofs of the love and presence of God as a Saviour among us in the conversion of our children. In the thirty-one years during which I have now been a city pastor, and personally connected with large schools, I have

received to the Lord's table over three hundred youth of both sexes, directly from the
Sunday-school. And I have no doubt I might
with equal truth add two hundred more, unit-
ing with us from the resulting influence of
previous Sunday-school instruction. This
is doubtless a great and blessed result, which
must give joy in the kingdom of God for ever.
Yet it has hardly been one in ten of the children to whom I have seen these priceless
blessings dispensed, and over whose favored
youth I have watched as a pastor. An early
revival in St. Paul's church in Philadelphia,
commenced in our weekly Sunday-school
prayer-meeting on Saturday evening. The
exercises closed, and the people were dis-
missed, when, rising from my place, I counted
sixteen of our youth still on their knees on the
floor. They were apparently immovable from
their position, and in deep emotion. I went
from one to the other with a few words of
affectionate and pastoral conversation, and
appointed Monday evening as an occasion for
their special assembly. On the next day I

gave notice of this appointment, and over seventy youth met me for instruction and prayer. It was the divine commencement of a very remarkable work of mercy. The result was the addition of over one hundred, mostly from the Sunday-school, to the communion of the Church. The subjects of that work are now active and earnest Christians, in the maturity of grace. Many such results, upon a narrower scale, have I since witnessed, and in every class of society, in connection with our Sunday-schools. I was called, in Philadelphia, to visit a sick girl in a very worldly and irreligious household, with whom I had but little acquaintance—and went, anticipating only a painful visit of warning to a careless soul. To my astonishment, I found a gentle child of grace, perhaps eighteen years of age, sinking in a consumption, but perfectly clear in mind, and happy in hope. "How," I asked, "have you learned all this in your condition here?" Her answer was most precious. "I had a faithful Sunday-school teacher—and though I left her some years ago, and never gave her much satisfaction, yet when I was taken sick, I took my little Bible, and went over the lessons she used to teach me—and God has taught me here alone." She then showed me her little Bible—turned down and marked with many Sunday-school lessons— her constant and loved companion. Dear child—she had no other religious companion. But she departed in sweet peace and hope— and my visits to her while she lived were full of satisfaction and delight. Similar instances of actual conversion under Sunday-school instruction have occurred in such numbers that I might fill many sheets of paper with them. I have seen them manifested in children from six years old and upwards; infants giving a clear account of their hope in Jesus, and love to Him—and thus, according to the promise of the Spirit, "perfecting His praise." I have seen whole families brought to Christ under such influence, who were far off from all Christian habits even, until little ones carried home from the Sunday-school the life-giving messages of truth. I have seen most interestesting exhibitions of deep and real religious fervor and faithfulness in the actual instruction; teachers and children really alive to their work, and completely engaged in its enjoyment. But as I have marked these blessed results, demonstrated possible and within reach, my heart has longed to see a constant and extended manifestation of such Divine influence in this youthful congregation. When I have looked upon them in their gathering and occupation, and spread before my anxious mind the value of their youth, the preciousness of their opportunities, the peculiar advantages of their assembly, the direct promises and illustrations connected with the young, and seen what might be attained in all, from what had been attained in so many, I have often been disturbed and overwhelmed by the want of real efficiency and vital power connected with the occupation. I have doubted whether the real expectation and object in the teachers' minds were the conversion of the souls of children. How precious has appeared that short hour of instruction! How import-

ant every impression which was to be made
on those open and plastic minds ! And when
levity or carelessness have occupied the place
of deep seriousness and concern in the little
assemblies around me, and teachers and children have appeared listless, or indifferent, or
trifling, I confess my soul has sunk in many a
moment of despondency and distress. I have
longed for a seriousness and solemnity, connected with cheerfulness and agreeable relations on the teachers' part, which would indicate their apprehension of the unspeakable
importance of their employment, and value of
the influence to be exercised. The work has
often had a tendency to run into a mere amusement, and the desire to make it attractive and
popular tends to throw a worldly and secular-
izing influence around it. It is sad to think
that we have often failed in obtaining the real
blessing, in the playful and light character
which we have given to the occupation, and
have sacrificed to superficial enjoyment the
more lasting happiness of real conversion.

IV.

 feel encouraged and grateful for the apparent acceptance and interest which have welcomed my hurried attempts to comply with your original request. The subject is very extensive and has a great variety of connections. Should I attempt to touch them all, my few familiar letters would swell into a volume. The single point now suggested, the advantages we have a right to expect from a faithful cultivation of this important work, spreads out into a variety of topics for consideration. I have said we have a right to expect the conversion of our children. Upon this point I would not be unintelligible or indefinite—by conversion, I mean the real spiritual turning of the heart to God, and its renewal for His service by the Holy Spirit.

This is the only actual starting of true Christian character : the new creation of the soul in Christ. Now, I suppose, a faithful Christian teacher will propound this to himself as an object. It will direct his prayers, his preparations, his methods of communication, and all his personal influence and intercourse with his children. He will labor for this great result until he gain it. He will not be satisfied without it. I do not mean that he shall occupy his time with mere exhortation to his class. Still less that he shall adopt a vehement and imperious style of address in his work—a manner which I have sometimes seen running into uncomfortable noise and actual disturbance. The instrument of conversion with children is the same as with adults—the Word of truth, the simple message of redeeming love. This message speaks in the simplest language in the sacred Word, and is perfectly intelligible to the youngest mind, nay, I often think far more so than to elder and more bewildered understandings. And if this message of actual pardon in the Saviour's blood, real

4

salvation through His death for all who will receive it, is placed before the youthful minds as
designed for them and belonging to them, with
the evidence of sincerity and earnestness on the
teacher's part, we may as reasonably look for a
blessing to attend the truth in the experience
of children as of adults. I call this expectation a right, because it seems to me the subject of divine promise; and that which God
has promised, we have an undoubted right to
ask and to expect. To this one great point
every lesson should be brought, and with every
child. The full attainment of this result, under the divine blessing, does not imply extra-
ordinary powers or education on the teacher's
part, but a real living experience of the power
of the truth, and love of the Word of God,
an earnest desire for the salvation of those to
whom it is offered, with a real belief that they
can be, and ought to be saved, under its min-
istration. This constitutes the adaptation of
the ministry in the pulpit, and is equally the
instrument of blessing for precious souls in the
Sunday-school.

I have constantly had before me very blessed illustrations of such fidelity and usefulness ; teachers to whom education, piety, and industrious preparation have combined to give great efficiency for their work, and whose earnest and religious habit and character have made them most attractive and popular among the youth before them. I have seen Bible-classes, both male and female, in which there was a constant pressure of attendance, and an outward desire to become partakers of the benefits there received, just as earnest. An intelligent, earnest, and instructed teacher, with a mind and heart engaged in the blessed work thus undertaken, believing in its value and influence, and determined to carry out that influence, with the Lord's blessing and Spirit, to the utmost, will always be popular and always efficient. Scholars will be punctual and happy, and God the Saviour will never be found slack in His promise of a blessing from heaven upon His Word. He will sanctify them through His truth. Such teachers make their mark in the history of the Church, and are held in abiding remembrance.

An eminent instance of this, was John Farr, of Philadelphia. He was a native of London, and a chemist of practical wisdom and success in business. He was one of our Bible-class teachers at St. Paul's—a model of a Sunday-school teacher. Truly spiritual, thoroughly evangelical, deeply earnest, never wearied, always attractive, he made his class to be considered by young men an invaluable privilege. God blessed his labors with increasing manifestations of divine grace and power. Young men now energetic and active in their maturity, in every class of the laborers in the Church of God, would to-day rise up and call him blessed. I have no doubt if all who found the Saviour under his earnest, constant fidelity, were called to stand together as witnesses for him, more than one hundred young men would appear to testify for him before the Lord. And yet I speak of only a portion of his labor in this cause. Who can estimate the full result for them, for the Church, for the world, of such labors as his? Yet never was there perhaps a Christian man more unpretending, unobtrusive, or simple-hearted than he. He has long since entered into his rest in the Saviour's glory. God grant to all his scholars grace to hold on in following him to the end.

A lovely young female teacher was taken from us at twenty-two years of age. She joined us as a teacher at sixteen, and labored with us but few years before her crown was given to her. Yet her whole class of girls, crowded always, seemed to listen to her with hearts perfectly absorbed, and felt the privilege of being taught by her one of the greatest joys of their life. Her fidelity in speaking for Jesus seemed never to fail. An evening's walk or a casual meeting would bring out something from her that would be a blessing to others. Her household, her friends, all felt the power of her religion. More than one young man of her acquaintance traced his conversion to her faithfulness. I had reason to believe that at least twenty-five youth around her, and I know not how many more, for my opportunity of knowledge was partial, were saved by the Lord's blessing upon her short but lovely min-

4*

istry... Yet there was nothing that was remarkable in her condition or education, beyond the common reach of young ladies in moderate circumstances of life. Her power was her religion, her fidelity to Christ. She was a real, living follower of the Saviour whom she loved, and for whom alone she lived. How brightly shine these examples and memories of the departed ! How encouraging to our earnestness and fidelity are their histories ! What a joy to a pastor's heart are the answers given by inquiring youth in reference to their own awakening, which in these two cases came to me from many, "It was Mr. Farr, or Miss ——, who first spoke to me, and aroused my mind to think of Christ." How paltry and sinful would seem any jealousy on the part of ministers, of such labors and success. I do not refer to living illustrations of this fidelity, though I might do so. The past furnishes evidence enough.

Now this whole view of the work also gives the utmost encouragement in our observation of its actual effect on the minds of youth.

Here I must only speak of the past and of those who are gone. I call to mind a dear child in our Sunday-school, whose early death, perhaps at sixteen years of age, sealed a beautiful testimony for Christ. My frequent visits to her chamber of intense suffering were full of comfort and delight. Such was her bodily agony that she could not lie down, or hardly sleep. But her soul was full of light and joy. Yet her teaching had been gathered, perhaps wholly, in the Bible-class and church. At one visit she said to me, " My precious pastor, listen to me. This is the way, I think. First, God the Father loved me, and chose me for His child ; then God the Son loved me, and came and died for me that I might be His child. Then God the Holy Ghost loved me, and came and told me I was His child, and made me love Him as His child. My precious pastor, is this right ?"

Blessed child of heaven, flesh and blood had not revealed it to her, but the Spirit of her Father in heaven. On another visit she said, " My precious pastor, I have had such a sweet

half-night of prayer—no, perhaps only a third
of the night. And I have been praying for
you, and for your dear son, that a double portion of the Spirit may rest upon him—and for
our dear Epiphany (my Philadelphia church),
that God would raise them up a faithful pastor, and for St. George's, that you may be
made as great a blessing to them as you have
been to us. And I thought I should love to
be with you in St. George's. You know I do
not know anybody there, but I shall always
love them because you are there. And then I
thought, after I am gone, if I were permitted,
I should ask Jesus to let me visit you in that
dear church." Much more she added in the
same strain, just as fresh in my memory, but
this is enough. She sat upon her bed with
her head leaning forward upon her knees, and
her hands clasped around them. At another
visit I found her sitting much in the same pos-
ture in an easy chair. She said " My precious
pastor,"—she never addressed me by any other
title—" I have had such a sweet dream of
heaven last night. Do you remember 'the

little sermon you preached to us about Sweet
Words and Bitter Words? Well, I thought
the language of heaven was made up of all the
sweet words of earth, and there were no bitter
words there, and it seemed so lovely to have
everybody speak to me so." These are a few
scraps from a multitude of memories of that
lovely child of God. Her faithful teacher is
still living, and has even perhaps a fuller
memory and a fuller joy than I in this relation.

These are illustrations of actual results.
They are deeply interesting, but not peculiar.
Every really flourishing Sunday-school can
furnish them. Every pastor, alive in this
work, has such sheaves in his bosom. Every
earnest, praying teacher will probably have
some similar testimony. They are but some
that have occurred to my mind while I have
been writing this letter. Memory will perhaps
recall many others. But these illustrate the
great purpose and the rightful result of our
teaching in the Word of God. Why should
it be thought a thing incredible, that God

should do this for our children ? Rather,
why should we not expect it, labor for it, anticipate it, as the natural, practical result ?
This blessed result may come in a variety
of manifestations, not always suddenly, not
always immediately, not always with much
observation. Sometimes after long trying
of faith, and prayer, and patience. Sometimes after the actual connection of the
teacher and the scholar has been sundered.
But its possibility, its likelihood, its certainty in God's own time and way, leads us
to pray, and labor, and teach, in the hope of
this one result. The purpose and expectation
give new energy and life to all our efforts.
The plan of instruction thus designed, mingles
a precious influence with all our words and
thoughts. Solemn, tender, affectionate, sincere—our children feel and see that we are so.
Their attention is arrested. Their thoughts
are awakened. Their minds are all alive. Ah,
how blessed is such a sight, and such an operation ! How full of joy and pleasure the
work so imbued and sanctified becomes ! And

how much every pastor loses who is not in it, and alive to it, and earnest for it, as one not only of the great but of the greatest interests of his ministry and office, as a shepherd of the flock, and an embassador for Christ.

LATER RESULTS.—TWO DIFFERENT CASES.—DYING CHILDREN.
—LOVE OF CHILDREN FOR SUNDAY-SCHOOL.—EFFECTS ON
FAMILIES.—HOME TEACHING.

THE advantages which we may anticipate from our Sunday-schools are by
no means exhausted in the one idea of
conversion. Assuredly the salvation
of our children is our great cardinal
purpose. But in the attainment of this, we
also attain many other important and blessed
results in detail. And even if we fail in this,
we have still many very precious facts of actual
gain. When we speak of conversion in any
case as connected with means to be employed
by men, we must not forget the sovereignty of
grace and the right of God to do what He will
with His own. It may be that the most earnest and faithful teacher may be disappointed—
may experience that hope long deferred which

maketh the heart sick. We must not allow ourselves to confine the attainment of this result to the limited time of Sunday-school teaching. The incident related in one of my former letters may illustrate a blessing coming long after the day of teaching has passed, and after the teacher's heart had felt, and even forgotten, all the despondency of the disappointment. Many cases have been under my notice of the blessing upon faithful teaching long postponed, and yet at last, even in maturity, crowning the work. And I have no doubt a very large proportion of all the conversions we see in the Church might be traced, if we knew all the facts, to the Scriptural knowledge laid up in the youthful mind by faithful teaching. The incorruptible seed of the Word may lie beneath the ground through a long winter of hopeless indifference and crime, and yet furnish the inestimable instrument of divine power, when the moment comes that God shall mercifully speak it into life and growth. And this laying up of knowledge for the future quickening work of the Spirit is a most important benefit which faithful teaching confers. The certainty of this may lead a praying, anxious teacher to have long patience, doubting not that in due season he shall reap if he faint not. Two young persons once sought my pastoral counsel in much the same circumstances, and about the same time. They were both young men, who had led a vain and wasteful life— living in pleasure, and dead while they lived. The one had been the child of early faithful Christian teaching. The other had known nothing in his childhood but the miserable worldliness of a Sabbath-breaking family, and an utter neglect of the Word of God. The Holy Spirit had now awakened both to personal anxiety and religious concern. They were deeply affected and manifestly sincere. But how different were their experience and their future history. The one instantly and freely embraced a truth which he had always known, and never doubted. It was all he desired—enough for him. He was fixed in judgment, actual in conviction, and useful in result. The salvation of the Gospel was to him a fountain of real and immediate blessedness, and he delighted to proclaim it. The other had no knowledge—was ignorant, skeptical, full of mental errors and absurd objections, and could never be settled or satisfied in mind or established in heart. The Word of God was all unknown to him, and he had never been trained to receive its authority. Not one conversation with him was satisfactory, and the toil of leading him was intense. I traced them long, and as I have marked the simple, cheerful, earnest life of the one—and the wayward, fitful, unhappy course of the other, I have but seen in every step of their career the benefit and blessedness of that early teaching in the Word of God in the Sunday-school, which made all the difference in their parallel courses. Yet perhaps in this most favored case, some praying teacher had often wept in disappointment over the apparent want of success of his labor as it passed.

But apart from these absolute advantages of spiritual knowledge, we confer benefits in our Sunday-schools of immense value, and to

be considered secondary only in comparison of
this first and highest of all blessings to man.
We gain the affections of children on the side
of the Gospel, and its institutions and instruction. Everything connected with religion assumes an attractive and agreeable aspect, and
approaches them under a new and most sub-
duing form. The love and kindness of a faithful teacher kindle a glow of personal affection
and tenderness, sometimes hardly second to
any other. To be the object of constant affectionate approach and address—to hear the language of tenderness and friendly salutation
only and always, awakens a living and often
an entirely new spirit in a youthful mind.
How often have I seen the most obdurate-look-
ing boy quietly yielding, like melting snow, to
such an influence, till he awoke to the real
feeling for the first time in his life, that he
was truly loved by somebody, and truly loved
somebody in return. How often have I known
a dying child exclaim, "Oh send for my
teacher ; I want to see my teacher,"—and this
in repeated cases of even infant scholars, sup-

posed too young to have derived deep and lasting impressions from this relation. Many
illustrations in facts occurring, rise up to my
mind in demonstration of this influence and
result, so valuable, that I should be ready to
say they alone were worth all the effort and
toil which the school had cost. So blessed is
this influence of love on the human heart, that
its worth as a refining power can not be overes-
timated. A Sunday-school teacher has an instrument of vast usefulness in this personal
relation, the effect of which, properly directed
and improved, it would be vain to calculate.

The affections of children are equally gathered around the Sabbath, the Church, the
Word of God, and the pastor also, if he sin-
cerely throw himself into the work, and minister to its prosperity. The Sabbath, no longer
a weariness, becomes to the mind of youth the
most attractive of all days. It is a day of enjoyment and pleasure. "Oh how I love to
have the Sabbath come," said a plain little
child to me, "it is so pleasant—and I love my
school so much." "The happiest hours of my

5*

whole week to me, are those I spend in the
Sunday-school," said another of an elder class.
What scores of little ones have I known coming in the cold winter mornings, with no breakfast, because their families were not up, and
they could not be satisfied to wait and lose
their school. "How came you here so soon?"
said I to two little girls of a rich and self-in-
dulgent household, who on a winter's morning
had come a great distance, and were the first
in the room. "Oh we love to come, and we
got up very early, and came without our breakfast, that we might not be late." "Freddy,"
said I to a little boy, "have you had your
breakfast to-day?" "No, sir, but I do not
mind that; I had much rather be at school."
Now, I say it is all but an infinite blessing,
thus to attract the youthful affections around
the Sabbath and the study of the Word of
God. Public worship and the privileges connected with the sanctuary are thus imbedded
in the youthful habits and tastes. A direction
and current are given to the thoughts and associations, which go far to take all stumbling-

blocks out of the Lord's way, and to make
ready a people prepared for the Lord. The
ministry become objects of deep and abiding
affection, if the pastor enters into the work.
The hearts of children are entwined around
him, as a well known minister to their joys.
His voice is familiar. His words are effective.
His memory is precious to them. Upon this
particular point, however, I shall not enlarge
more at present. But what a hold, what a
vantage-ground, have we gained, if we can
thus make all the arrangements and institutions of religion objects of pleasant and attractive associations in youthful minds ! We
give a happy youth, and we prepare for a
happy maturity. We minister in a most
effectual manner for the future work of the
Spirit, by clothing all the appointed instruments of that work with only pleasurable
associations.

Now, teachers can trace this influence and
its effects in every Sunday-school in our land,
in which the Word of God is simply and faithfully taught. And it is an influence only to

be gained in Sunday-schools. Domestic religious teaching can never confer these agreeable
associations to the church, the pastor, or the
Sabbath. On the contrary, the most earnest
of Christian parents have always found the
Sabbath family work a hard work—and the
Sabbath family teaching a wearying teaching.
Well do we, who passed our youth with only
the teachings of a Christian home, realize this.
And while memory blesses and consecrates
those venerable and beloved forms of parents
long departed, who were serious, earnest, conscientious, prayerful—yet the remembrance of
our Sabbaths, with nothing to call out youthful affection, or awaken youthful earnestness,
or enlist youthful waywardness, or to turn our
desires to pastors whom we never knew, or to
worship which we could not understand, is,
after all, far from a green spot in the recollec-
tions of youth. There are needed, for the best
instructed, all the additional facts of provision
which our Sunday-schools have given us—not
to supplant, but to supplement domestic teaching, and the care and nurture of a Christian

home. And the wisest Christian parents now
fully understand this. The attempt to create
a rivalry or antagonism between parental domestic teaching and the teaching of the Sunday-school, is evidence to us only of ignorance
of the subject. The one may give the advantages of solitary religious teaching. The other
alone engrafts upon this, and adds to this the
social benefits and opportunities of pleasant .
religious relations and religious influences in
association. Accordingly, the perfect scheme
and the perfect operation are only to be found
in the combination of the two. I have had
the contrast in families equally under my pastoral care. And I have sadly felt the impos-
sibility of gaining the affection of children
whom I had with me in no other relation than
the family. Many families have I seen who
were fixed in the sentiment, that the Sunday-
school was not needful for their children, and
that even greater benefits would be lost by
sending them thither. The simple result has
been, that these children, though in some cases

belonging to Christian parents, and, I believe,
conscientiously instructed at home, have grown
up free from any influence of mine, or of the
ministry, or of desire therefor, and, as a rule,
voluntary strangers in maturity, to the blessings of a day and a Church which they had
never been accustomed to love in their youth.
I have mourned over this error, in occasional
determinations, with exceeding sorrow—long-
ing to see every child and youth in the Church
in actual, constant connection with blessings
which I have been perfectly convinced could
elsewhere never be supplied. I would entreat Christian parents to feel and to consider rightly upon this subject ; and, while in
their prayers and efforts at home and in secret,
they seek for the highest spiritual welfare of
their children, to perceive and acknowledge
how blessed and valuable is that helpful agency
which the good providence of God has prepared
for their aid and success in the Sunday-school.
Here are advantages in which they are vitally
interested. Let them adopt them, and seek

a divine blessing upon them, for their own households, rejoicing in their connection with churches and ministers, where such faithful teaching is arranged, and privileges so precious for youth are prepared.

VI.

THE incidental advantages of Sunday-schools, which occupied my last letter, are a very interesting subject to me. I can not substitute them in my mind as a satisfactory result in the place of real conversion, an actual living for Christ by the teaching and power of the Holy Spirit. But I can not bring myself to undervalue them, even as an object, much less as an instrument of great value toward the attainment of our ultimate and desired end. It is everything with me to attract the affections, and engage the thoughts and efforts of our children with religious interests and teaching. A teacher who can do this may be a vast instrument of abiding benefit. A teacher who can not, will accomplish but little, however earnest and serious he may be. Accordingly, I set a high value upon these contingent benefits, and delight to enumerate them as I see them constantly arising in connection with our schools.

In addition to those of which I have already spoken, the refinement of manners, tastes, and character which arises from our Sunday-school system and instruction, is a most precious benefit. I remember that Dr. Dwight does not hesitate to enumerate among the benefits flowing from the Sabbath, the refinement of habit and character which comes from the habitual weekly cleanliness and dress of the people upon that day. This thought has been always impressed upon me in connection with our Sunday-schools, as particularly valuable. If education in our public and common schools constantly awakens dormant character and powers—as we well know—the additional influence of the great subject of teaching, of the freeness and kindness of the manner of teaching, of the instinctive regard to the holiness of the day—of the religious worship in praise and prayer connected with it—and of all the circumstances of order and cleanliness in dress and habit which are especially required and seen on the Sabbath, give to our Sunday-schools an immense preponderance over all others in this relation. I have seen so much of this effect, and such power exercised by these schools in thus elevating and refining the poor, that I could fill many letters with instances illustrating the fact. Our missionary and pastoral biographies are full of these trophies of Divine grace, exhibiting this taking of children from the very poorest of the people, to make them princes in the Church of God in all lands—noble and commanding intellects that but for the first opening to daylight which the Sunday-school furnished, might have remained for ever hidden and unknown.

In one of our large public institutions is an accomplished professor of languages who came a poor boy to my school. His parents had no means of advancing him. He had displayed no particular taste for attainment. His associations had been far down below the prospect

of any possible elevation. The Sunday-school
brought out his hidden fire, and stirred up the
gift that was in him ; excited the desire for an
education ; led him to give himself and his education to God. He struggled through his
youth with the noble purpose before him. He
found friends in his Sunday-school connection to sustain him. He graduated with the
highest collegiate honors. He was able to educate and exalt his whole family. Few who
now know and admire him, have the least idea
where was found the spark of that brilliant exhibition. Yet it was the Sunday-school which
took him out of the dust, and inspired him
with all his early thoughts and plans. And
he has been a faithful teacher in this work
through all his manhood since.

A little girl of ten years old, perhaps, found
her way as one of our scholars. She lived as
" a little maid," like the one that waited on
Naaman's wife, in a rich but careless family,
who went to no church and kept no Sabbath.
In the few succeeding weeks after she came
among us, she brought with her one and an-

other of the children of the household, till she succeeded in attracting every child in the family to the school. The father and mother followed, and took a pew in the church. The final result was the adding to our communion both parents and children, as one of the happiest and most faithful families I have known. The little girl was so excited and taught in the Sunday-school that she longed for a thorough education. She was permitted by the family to attend the public school. She rose to be an assistant and a principal teacher. A distant town, about organizing a new public female school of a higher order, sent to the trustees of these public schools for a teacher thoroughly qualified to take this important post. They unanimously recommended our "little maid," and she was appointed. She has since been at the head of another more important institution, and has now educated hundreds of young ladies, who were never called to toil, nor knew the pressure of want. I could give many particulars of her remarkable course. But it was the Sunday-school that elevated and refined her, in character, desires, and plans. Apparently, but for the opening which was presented there, she might have spent her weary life in the mere service of the kitchen.

Who can undervalue such influences and results as these? Such instances, both male and female, might be multiplied from my own observation to an indefinite extent. Probably every Sunday-school and pastor could adduce parallel illustrations. They are the legitimate results of our work. They flow in the natural process of our plan and growth. I have some living instances now around me equally remarkable. I almost doubt whether any of our scholars entirely lose, or fail to gain, this refining influence of our schools in some degree. The mingling of the rich and poor produces a blessed equalizing influence upon both. A visitor to my school once said to me, " You seem to have no poor children here." I answered, " Nearly half of the children present are entirely poor." He looked at a class of girls who were near us, and expressed his doubts. I said, " See those two seated first on the bench. One of them is the daughter of a man of large wealth, the other the child of a poor widow who supports her family with her needle." "I see no difference between them," was his reply. Such was the aspect. And such is the elevating and refining power of our schools when made attractive and effective.

Another very important result of our work is the giving of religious information and benevolent purposes and habits. The missionary world is habitually spread out before them. The influence and history of Christian missions is now almost an inseparable part of the Sunday-school work. They are trained to consider this great subject, and to feel a lively interest in it. Thus not only are the missionary ranks supplied from the Sunday-schools, but all our benevolent operations find their laborers there, and the funds for all these works are thus habitually and freely raised. This whole department of interest and information has arisen in the time of us who are old. But what a work it is. Our children have grown up in the midst of the greatest triumphs of the Gospel, and are to a great degree familiar with them. They love to hear of them. They love to contribute to them. They are coming into the action of life, a well-informed army of soldiers for the Lord—"bayonets that think," as Kossuth called his revolutionary soldiers. Their views, expectations, and plans, are all arranged on a new and higher scale than has governed with those who have gone before them. The future victories of the Gospel will all be the victories of the Sunday-school. There were the men and women drilled and taught who "shall inherit the earth." The habit of missionary collections on every Sunday is a very important element of this department of influence. These even in themselves will amount to much. In the past ten years the missionary contributions of the Sunday-schools of St. George's have amounted to over Twenty Thousand dollars, collected in the schools, and by and from the children and teachers. These have erected a large stone church in Monrovia in Africa, which they are now finishing, and a very fine and commodious mission chapel in their own district of this city, which is finished and occupied, and has been highly successful. The children thus see the result of their labors. They are animated with new zeal and interest in the work. They gain new power and new tastes and habits as they go on in this work of benevolence from year to year. And the amount of money they collect is the smallest item of advantage in this one part of the operation. With what hope may we look forward to the influence and labors in the Church, of children so brought up and so habituated, to attempt large things, and to expect large things, for their Saviour and their fellow-men. I would encourage, therefore, all who are ready to work in this great cause, with the hope and animation which these facts and considerations may impart. I speak of all these things as advantages which we have a right to expect from our Sunday-schools, and, therefore, as ends and objects which in their several measure and relation we may and ought to pursue. Perhaps on this one point I have said enough. It has only suggested, however, much more which I am compelled to omit.

VII.

HOPE you will not think that I have arrayed an extravagant view of the advantages of our Sunday-schools to the children engaged in them. I am perfectly sure that I have but stated that which every well-conducted school and every faithful teacher in our land can more or less certify by their own observation and history. As a result of my experience and observation the exhibition is far within the line of truthful application, in the variety of incidents and instances with which I might substantiate it. But it is varied and adequate, sufficiently for all my present purpose. And in contemplating this area of thought, I am ready to ask, Can there be a cause, or an instrument of blessing, in the Church of God, of more real

and vital importance to its prosperity ? Has
the divine Providence given us a power or an
opportunity more adapted by His blessing to
glorify the Saviour's name, and to gather souls
in a spiritual fellowship and devotion to Him ?
The living power of the Church is to be perpetuated in its living posterity. The generations to come are to serve and bless the Lord
—in the extending of their power, and in the
enlarging of their capacity for the work of
Christ upon the earth. We do not doubt that
periods are rapidly approaching of the history
of the Church of Christ, which are to be distinguished by a zeal for truth, a love for Jesus,
and a laborious devotion to the best interests
of men, far beyond anything that we have seen
—perhaps that any Christians have yet ever
seen—of the glory, fullness, and power of the
Gospel. In anticipation of these days of vic-
tory, what is so important as the conversion
and Christian training of the young—the im-
buing them with a deep experience of the
power, and with large views of the promises
and prospects of the Gospel ? Not merely

bringing them personally, actually to Christ,
but also preparing them in the best and most
effectual way to work for Christ, in the gathering in of His great harvest of glory in the
salvation of men. Certainly the Church which
can be most effectually successful in this real
Christian training of the children belonging to
them, is the one most truly preparing to meet
their God, and to work for Him as a willing
people in the day of His power. And how is
this thorough Christian training to be accomplished upon any other plan than our Sunday-
school arrangement? I think I have sufficiently illustrated this point to assume it, and
leave it as indubitable. There is no rival operation. There is no comparable instrument.
There is no agency to take the place of this
great work even in the most partial degree.
And if one could imagine the whole effort to
be relinquished, and every Sunday-school to be
finally closed and scattered on a given day, with
all the aids and publications connected with
them to be thrown away, we can not conceive
a greater disaster to the Church, a greater tri-

umph of Satan, or a greater overthrow of the hope of a world redeemed.

The benefits of this work we are already reaping in the whole display of a Saviour's triumphs in the world. The present generation of youthful pastors and missionaries, and of male and female teachers and laborers, are chiefly the children of Sunday-school instruction. And, as the whole practical efficiency of the Church is yearly enlarging, and missionaries at home and abroad are hastening to publish upon the mountains the glad tidings of a reigning Saviour, we discover in this whole work but the precious fruit, shaking like Lebanon, of that which was thus scattered as a handful of corn, in the early efforts of the first faithful laborers in this cause. And when you contemplate the usefulness of many of these youthful servants of the Lord, some of whom have finished their day, and others of whom are still in the field, all of whom have been shining examples of the power and skill which this blessed training gave—and then call to mind the *three millions* of children in

our Churches in this country, now under all
the blessed influence of the same preparation
for Christ and His service, you can not resist
the thought, that nothing can be more important for the Church of God than the wise and
faithful maintenance of this whole scheme,
upon the largest possible field, and with the
utmost possible excellence of management.
Are there in this country five hundred thousand other Christians, of equal usefulness and
worth with the five hundred thousand Sunday-
school teachers whom God is employing and
blessing on every Sabbath ? Their whole employment in this relation, and in the degree
in which it is faithfully carried out—is the
highest gift of benevolence to our land and to
our race. It is a benevolence which continually enlarges itself in the heart that owns and
exercises it, which accomplishes the most
valued results for the souls upon whom it
directly acts, and which reproduces itself in
countless other agents and agencies, running
on through all ages, and intertwining with all
works of love, in the whole extent and history

of the future Church. And I would hail and welcome, my beloved brethren and sisters, the Sunday-school teachers of our country with the salutation of cordial affection and sincere respect. Beloved, you are the Lord's instruments of untold benefits to your fellow-men. Ages shall rise up and call you blessed. Be faithful unto death,—work on cheerfully and earnestly, and with a single mind; and the God of glory will endow you with eternal blessing. Be not wearied with apparent want of success, nor faint under the depression of hope deferred. You serve a faithful Master. You labor in a cause that is purely good and must surely triumph. You shall reap your harvest of grace and glory in due season, if you faint not.

But with the survey of this whole field of undeniable advantages accruing from our schools, what ought, what can our Churches do, but encourage, adopt, and sustain the work with the utmost devotion, generosity, and zeal? Christian pastors can not neglect this subject, and be useful, safe, or guiltless.

God has committed to His ministers the feeding of the lambs, as of the sheep.   The Son
of God made special manifestations of His
love, His peculiar love, for the little ones of
His flock.   And that can not be a ministry
faithful to God, or a ministry after the pattern of Jesus, which neglects them.   A Christ-
loving pastor is a child-loving pastor.   He who
as a babe has been taught of Jesus, delights to
be a teacher of babes for Jesus' sake.   A loving minister's heart can not withhold himself
from this most attractive and precious portion
of all his labors.   And I am persuaded that
the more the ministers of the Lord look at
this subject in all its bearings and influences,
the more earnestly will they be drawn to a personal engagement therein.   Christian Churches
can not be safely indifferent or inattentive to
these important claims.   The children of every
family, whether rich or poor, need the training
of the Sunday-school, and can gain the blessings which it offers nowhere else.   It should
be a fixed- purpose and effort in every Church
that the whole generation of its youth should

be thus taught and trained. There the rich and poor should meet together in the enjoyment of that elevating and refining influence which proceeds alone from Him who is "the Maker of them all." The best intellects and hearts of the Church of God should be given to this work. The teaching should not be confined to the young. Elder Christians, of long experience and mature grace, of commanding position and personal influence, should enlist themselves in the actual work— and renew their energies and their youth in the attractive labor to which it invites. The provision for the schools should bring out the unsparing liberality of the Church. Nothing that can promote the comfort, enlarge the usefulness, or adorn and render attractive the method of operation, within the power of the members of any Church, should be withheld. The Sunday-school is worthy of the first place in the affections and consideration of every Church. The advantages which it repays make it an investment of incalculable worth. In no way can the Churches of the Lord so surely rise and shine, so certainly extend and prosper, so largely bless and be blessed, as in the constant, earnest, and faithful cultivation of their Sunday-schools. They are the Church of the children—the fold for the lambs—the feeding-place for the kids beside the shepherds' tents. As true religion revives, the Lord makes their peculiar claims to be understood and valued. And as their claims are thus regarded and met, will true religion revive in the most effective and abiding form, and children and teachers, and pastors and Christians, awake to perceive and acknowledge, with new gratitude, the advantages and blessings which, under God's gracious blessing, flow from the Sunday-schools upon every one engaged therein.

7*

VIII.

PASS from a consideration of the advantages to be derived from Sunday-schools, to a contemplation of the agency to be employed. The value of the proposed result makes the importance of the agency designed to produce it still the greater. The discriminate character of the results which we desire must also influence our selection of an agency entirely appropriate to their attainment. In the subject before us, the first element of the agency is the personal character of the Teacher. A more important influence, or one more actually effective upon the character of the Church, can not be found, apart from the personal work of the divinely appointed ministry of the Gospel, than the organized and active body of Sunday-school teachers. They

have advantages of influence which are peculiarly their own. The small number of their
hearers—their acknowledged personal relation
as teachers—the direct individual and mutual
contact and connection of this relation—the
quiet and secured attention—the secluded place
and hour for their work—the open and eager
minds of the young disciples whom they instruct—the facility of comprehension and the
freedom of impression—the solemnizing, sub-
duing, and exciting influence of the accom-
panying prayer and praise of the school united—all combine to give them an opportunity
of blessing and saving a generation for Christ,
which angels might covet, and over the blessed
results of which angels will rejoice. As I
habitually walk around among the classes,
and sometimes have an opportunity to take
the place of an absent teacher, and thus ob-
serve and test, in turn, the blessedness of opening the absorbing truths of salvation to such
open and grateful minds, I gain a constantly
enlarging conception of the privileges and
blessings of the work. No employment seems

to me so attractive—and no occupation so
sure to bring its ample reward. That blessed·
hour of free and unrestrained conversation, in
the simplest terms upon the highest subjects,
only appears too short for the privilege and
the occupation which are necessarily confined
to it. And in the supposition that every element involved in this occupation is of a fair
and full measure of adaptation to its successful accomplishment, I can conceive of no influence upon human society at all to be com-
pared in efficacy and actual power with the
scheme of operation which is thus considered.
I can not speak or think of this agency as ever
rivaling, or really separable from, the appointed
ministry. The teachers of my schools seem
to me to be but parts of myself. Like the fin-
gers of one of those beautiful power-presses,
they take up the very pages which I desire to
impress, and smoothly and quietly spread them
out before me, prepared to receive the blessed
communications from on high which I long to
stamp on their minds and hearts for ever.
When one surveys this tranquil but powerful

operation, it is vain to compare the parts with each other in their relative importance. They must all be there, all proportionate, all adapted, all in order ; and then the unseen, mysterious power applied, with its sure but imponderable energy, the result comes out, the happiness and the triumph of all. And who that stands to contemplate the glowing regularity and mysterious beauty of this work, would desire to go back to the single hand-press of the individual laborer, toiling, with far greater weariness, to accomplish but a small portion of the result ? That in actual practice we really find a fair exhibition of these appropriate elements I have no power to deny. The great proportion of teachers are doubtless useful and faithful. And the very existence and constant enlargement of the operation on all sides and in every Church, while every element is so voluntary and unconstrained, can not but show the adaptation of the actual agency, and the interest of youthful minds therein. The rule of the history is flourishing success. The exceptions are the failing and drooping schools, and

inattentive and careless attendants. Yet there
is no school in which there are not found very
great differences, both in the passing manifestation, and in the actual results, among the
various classes and teachers. Every school
will furnish some specimens of what may be
called the highest exemplification of the system; some classes always present, always
punctual, always interested, always active;
some teachers always there, always prepared,
always attractive, always effectual; and therefore some fruits of the highest and most blessed
character always growing. That this difference will be found in some degree among the
children I should not deny. But this can be
only occasional and individual. There are
teachers, too, who are found especially adapted
to some particular classes of children. But
the differences are just as great between the individual children of the same general class, as
between the social classes themselves. And
there are some teachers who are always instruments of blessing, and I might almost say a
blessing to all. How dear and precious such

servants of the Lord are to a pastor's heart, and to the welfare of the Church, who can fairly tell ? But why should not all be such ? There may be, and doubtless there is, difference of 'gifts. But are there any gifts calculated for usefulness in the Sunday-school that every teacher may not in a fair measure and degree acquire ? Are there any that every Christian may not have and exercise in some appropriate relation with entire success ? I think not. And therefore while I speak upon this subject, I must deal with it, not as involving only the characteristics of the poet, natural and not to. be attained, but as the qualifications of the faithful practical servant, whose best services are the improvements of his constant opportunities, and whose brightest graces are the light of a lamp which, though grace has started with its divine spark, faithful watching and care keep in its abiding and useful glow.

Of all qualifications in a successful teacher, real and experimental piety is by far the most important. A teacher in a Sunday-school actually and professedly unconverted, seems an anomaly simply absurd. I should hardly waste a moment in discussing such a point. "In this the children of God are manifest and the children of the devil." If there are but these two classes on earth, in a spiritual division, as I certainly can not doubt, I can hardly imagine the propriety of employing one of either class to be a teacher in the ways of the other. There surely may be true piety in its germ in the heart, where as yet no open profession of it has been made in appointed ordinances of separation. And a wise consideration by the appointing power will take this possible fact into consideration in the present contingency. Perhaps the very desire to teach others the ways of Christ may be one of the first and most encouraging evidences of the reality of this spiritual life within, however feeble and doubtful it may appear. I would not, therefore, quench the smoking flax, or break the bruised reed : nor on any account discourage one of the Lord's little ones in their desires to be useful. But it is a case which requires vast caution, and faithful and tender judgment. The interest to be confided is great. The possible evils may be greater. And all the circumstances which are individual and personal must be taken into account. But the governing principle must be laid down, that a teacher of others to be the children of God, should himself be His child ; a guardian and guide of the little children of the Saviour's household ought not to be a-stranger and foreigner, having no hope, and without God in the world, but a fellow-citizen with the saints, and of the household of God. True piety is the growth and fruit of a converted heart—an experience of the Saviour's forgiving love—a real consecration of the soul, as bought with a price, to Him who has redeemed and owns it. It is a state in which old things have passed away, and all things in their principles, and in their measure and degree of results, have become new. A Sunday-school teacher must be thus taught and born of God, so that the divine subjects of teaching shall not be the mere barren acquisitions of the hearing of the ear, but the real subjects of the experience and enjoyment of the heart. I am exceedingly earnest to press this point. It is the very starting-point in this new line of view. Every thing else will depend upon it, and presuppose it. We can not, therefore, pass it with indifference or inattention. What is Sunday-school teaching but a ministry for God? In the very nature of the employment, it is a work for Christians, and for them alone. The idea is sometimes suggested, that getting some vain and irreligious persons to teach others, may be the means of leading them to learn themselves. This would seem too wicked to be merely absurd, if applied to the ministry of the Gospel. But though more manageable and more easily remedied, it is equally incongruous in the present case. We can not afford to present our children as merely demonstrative subjects. Their interests and welfare are the things for which we seek. And in securing an agency for the blessing, the Lord must first call to His service, and then instruct and prepare for its adequate fulfillment. Our teachers must be in choice, and hearts, and life the children and servants of the living God.

IX.

TEACHERS.—RELIGIOUS KNOWLEDGE.—SCRIPTURAL KNOWL-
EDGE.—SPECIAL PREPARATION.—LOVE FOR SOULS.—EF-
FORTS FOR SALVATION.

HAVE spoken of piety as an essential qualification in a Sunday-school teacher. But the thought should be carried beyond the mere possession of religious character. For such a work there needs the deepest experience and intelligence of religious truth. It is really a ministry for souls in eternal things, and at a period of life when the impressions received are very permanent and effectual. False principles then inculcated may exercise a baneful influence through life. Indeed, it may be found very difficult to eradicate them at all. Nothing can be more important than to give to a youthful mind a perfectly clear and intelligible perception of the way of salvation opened in the Gospel. And though every true Christian will understand this, and may be able to state it with a degree of precision—at any rate must be personally conscious of its simplicity—yet it is by no means the fact that every real Christian can adequately and with sufficient simplicity expound it to others. To make it plain to a child's mind, even when that mind is really spiritually inquiring, is a very important attainment. It will occupy and will repay the ripest experience in grace, and the most intelligent exercise of wisdom. ' I have, therefore, always longed to see those Christians at work in teaching, who were not merely alive to God, but lively for God. We need the mature servants to be the guides of the young. And no employment is so adapted to invigorate their own graces, and to simplify and clear up their own views of Divine truth, as this opportunity and necessity of expounding the way of the Lord to His little ones, and showing them, in their own tongue, the wonderful works of God. How much the practical imparting of religious knowledge enlarges and purifies it in the mind's own possession, Christians in such an occupation would soon discover.

You will see that this whole train of remark is founded upon my previous assertion of the purpose of Sunday-school teaching—that is, the actual conversion of children to God. However important theoretical information may be in the geography and customs of Scripture history, it would be a miserable perversion of our appointed work to confine the time and thoughts to this outside view. A lesson in Scriptural geography alone would be as barren and as inappropriate in the Sunday-school as a sermon on the same subject in the pulpit. Both the one and the other are useless, and derogatory to the position and the demand, unless all the statistical information be made the instrument of direct introduction to the Saviour's work and the sinner's need. And although we must delight to welcome and employ every adjunct which enlarged information can bring to illustrate and explain the truth, we must be exceedingly determined and careful that the incident shall not assume the place of the very subject itself,

8*

and the chaff be selected for the food instead
of the wheat. A teacher truly alive for God
will soon and often find an opportunity to
confer with individual minds, upon the great
concerns of the Gospel and the sinful soul.
And it is eminently necessary that teachers
should realize the importance of a deep religious experience, and an habitual exercise of all
its active traits for the special advantage of
this work, and for readiness for such occa-
sions.

Added to this primary qualification, we may
speak, as second in importance, of enlarged
Scriptural knowledge. Every part of the Sacred Word should be familiar to a teacher's
mind. And to the utmost extent of individual means and time, the widest preparation
should be made of attainment from this whole
field. Here will come in the whole area of
study in the localities and national customs
which are connected with the historical teaching of the Bible. When we began our work,
this field for study was vastly extensive, and
widely scattered. But the laborers and prepa-

rations which the process of the work has called out, in the condensed and comprehensive books prepared upon these various points, have so simplified and arranged the study, that it involves but little difficulty now for any. But this knowledge is only to be acquired by study—and in the great multitude of cases, it can only be acquired by the actual study of the particular lesson. I have had great reason to believe there is far too little actual study on the appointed lesson by the most of teachers. In hurried and extemporaneous work in teaching I have no confidence. It is as worthless in the Sunday-school as in the pulpit. In each case it wearies and disgusts the speaker and the hearers equally. The Sunday's lesson should be the week's study. The reading and the thought should be given to it. Ample notes should be made of the information attained. And the teacher should come prepared to the utmost possible extent, with information on the whole subject, and the ability to answer any reasonable question, or to expound any natural difficulty which may occur. " Reading maketh a full man." And it is delightful to witness the work of such an one in teaching. The scholars crowd around and hang upon his words, and the excitement and occupation of the mutual interest in the subject of study, make the hour seem too short for both. How sad a contrast is the aspect of another class and teacher, where the little information of the teacher has been soon exhausted—and before the hour has half gone by, the teacher sits with folded hands in idleness, and the children are yawning with indifference, or else the Word of God is laid aside and some story-book is read in its place. We may mournfully think of Cowper's words in a similar case:

"From such apostles, oh ye mitred heads, preserve the Church,
And lay not careless hands on skulls that can not teach,
And will not learn."

The complaint is often made by teachers, we can not get our children to study the lesson. The interest of the children will always be dependent upon the teacher. If the teacher provides nothing to say, the children will look for nothing to hear. The previous study of the one will awaken the desire and study of the others. And it would be wholly unnatural to expect in the minds of youth a spontaneous and continued interest in the great subjects of Scriptural study, with no adequate or appropriate efforts to awaken and maintain it. I would entreat teachers to consider the importance of this study. What a blessing to their own souls would be one chapter of sacred Scripture thus thoroughly studied and understood, every week! What a fund of learning and truth would one year's work of this kind lay up for them! And how increasing and enlarging would become their power to teach, and their own ability to understand the Word of God, as years go by of such patient and compensating toil. In the increasing religious information of individual minds, the character and influence of the Church become proportionably enlarged, and the pulpit may be encouraged and enabled to speak of the deeper things of God, and the ministry grow in knowledge and in wisdom in imparting it.

In addition to these qualifications in teach-

ers, we want an active and earnest love for
souls—a sincere and positive desire for their
salvation. Love for souls must flow from love
for Him who bought them. The love of Christ
must be the constraining power to awaken and
sustain this feeling. The mind which was in
Him, is eminently needful for the Sunday-
school. We can hardly conceive of true religion that is indifferent to this object. But
there is evidently a vast difference among
Christians in active feeling concerning it. In
our teachers we must seek for this spirit—and
encourage and labor to bring it out. The
connection in which they are placed is equally
solemn and interesting. They are the messengers of Christ to these little ones. They are
employed to carry His glad tidings to them.
They may be employed to lead their ransomed
souls to Him. What element of usefulness is
more important to them than a real and earnest love for those to whom they minister?
It will labor in prayer for them. It will present them individually and by name before the
Lord, imploring His blessing. It will direct

their whole utterance in actual teaching. It will lead to an observation and understanding of their individual characters and particular temptations. It will visit them in their habitations—cultivate an affectionate intercourse with them—call out their personal confidence and grateful regard—and make the teacher known to them as their real and beloved friend. It will devise many and constant ways of interesting and attracting them. It will make the gaining them and blessing them for Christ a constant and real object of thought and effort. It is a blessed spirit, both as an instrument in the teacher's hand, and as a dweller in the teacher's heart. It must be sought, watched over, and encouraged by every teacher. And coldness or indifference here must be felt to be, as it really is, a great and dreadful evil—to be guarded against and repressed in every possible way, and by unceasing purpose and effort. But piety, deep experience in religion, extended Scriptural knowledge, and ardent love for souls, vast and precious as they are, do not finish a teacher's qualifications. We must still pursue this theme.

X.

HAVE desired to speak of the proper and essential qualifications in a Sunday-school teacher, with much moderation of expression. Those which we have considered have been attributes and attainments, which however they must vary in individual instances, are certainly within the reach, in a fair measure, of every real servant of the Lord Jesus. Native powers of mind, and social opportunities for education, will materially vary the degree of their possession. But there are equal varieties of children to be cared for and taught under their influence. And with reasonable wisdom and discernment in the appropriation of teachers on the part of the Superintendent, there will be found a place for every one, and an adapted field for the labors of all. As a rule in our experience in this work, I believe the testimony will be general, that we fail in bringing for its accomplishment the best talent and education in our Churches, and therefore are often compelled to work our great enterprise with inferior means and instruments, from the very necessity of the case. How this difficulty is to be met, but by an outpouring of the Spirit in new measure upon our Churches, I can not tell. I see around me Christian men and women of the highest character and position, who have every qualification for a successful union with us—so far as education and religious attainments go—who still withhold themselves entirely. There seems no love for souls, or confidence in the importance of this great means of salvation, adequate to overcome their personal convenience, or the indolence and self-indulgence of their tempers. They do not realize the great fact that we are really educating the Church of God in its coming generations, and have the vast responsibility and opportunity of impressing upon those who are to come, the great truths and principles of the Gospel—that we are therefore starting and supplying little streams of blessing, which may even in their own time flow down as mighty rivers of Divine mercy to mankind.

What blessings some teachers live to enjoy as the divinely bestowed fruits of their work ! A beloved missionary from Africa, who has now labored for eleven years on that dark shore, has just returned among us. He went from all the joys and luxuries of this city, in the morning of his ministry, to give himself to the Lord for that peculiarly self-denying work. He found on his present return his early Sunday-school teacher still at work in her important trust. This beloved missionary and another clergyman settled in this city, were two of her boys, when she gave herself, as a youth, with peculiar love and life to this important work. The youthful teacher has passed into the maturer age and circumstances of life, surrounded with her large family cares and calls—and yet she labors on with all the attraction of sanctified talent and loveliness of character, which early blessed, and still equally bless the generations of youth committed to her. How many there are around who might be equally useful, and equally happy in usefulness, with far more time at their command, could they attain the same love for the Saviour and His blessed work. This is a point on which I deeply feel, and often meditate with great distress. How shall I call out the best and most efficient talent in my Church in this cause? I can not doubt that the deficiency is a religious deficiency. The real defect is the want of living, earnest piety and love for Christ—gifts which the Holy Ghost can alone impart, and the bestowal of which will be the revival of His work in the Church.

But with the best agents we can find, we must labor still. It is with the Lord to save by many or by few. And we too often see our "calling" to be but the repetition of the Corinthian experience. The mighty, the noble, and the wise refuse the privilege, while God adorns and consecrates the weak things of the world to be mighty through Him, that they who glory, may glory in the Lord alone. The qualifications of which I speak must, therefore, have relation to things as they are. A very important addition to those of which I have already spoken, will be a really loving heart, affectionate and gentle habits—the cultivation of an attractive demeanor in relation to the children, and to fellow-teachers. This surely is a grace within the reach of every one, and is equally valuable to its possessor, and to those who are to feel its influence. No Christian employment more constantly or indispensably demands the law of kindness. And no talents or gifts can compensate here for a rough or un-kind deportment. The law of the Sabbath-school must be love. When often asked for the constitution and rules of my schools, I answer that they are comprised in the four let-ters, L O V E. Here is the law—and this the only fulfilling of the law, in a Sunday-school. I have more than once passed classes under my care, when a teacher has called to me to say, "Here is a ·boy or girl that I can do nothing

with ; can you not remove him or her to some
other class ?" Now, how manifest was the in-
competence of the teacher under such circumstances. Impatience, want of sympathy and
tenderness, to say the very least, were at the
bottom of the whole ; great want of discretion
in openly announcing the disappointment,
which was a confession of incompetency to the
whole class, and extremely injudicious and ir-
ritating to the child proscribed, was very apparent. Indifference to the feelings and convenience of fellow-teachers was equally clear.
In such a case, nothing could be done but to
remove the child. But I should have felt more
disposed to remove the teacher, if a greater result of evil would not have probably flowed
from it. A complaining teacher can do no
good. A fretful, peevish, hasty teacher can do
no good. If a child is rebellious, let a teacher
remember what fighters against God the ministry must meet ; and how surely every thing
will be unavailing in them all for a blessing,
without a forbearing, patient spirit. A smiling
genial habit, a cheerful, welcoming countenance

9*

—a morning face radiant with joy in the work of the Lord—comes into the school like the sunshine of heaven. It is God's own work, and God's own mark. I can not but say, "I will rejoice and be glad therein."

To cultivate the influence of this spirit, I feel the importance of teaching the two sexes in the same room. Indeed, for our smaller boys, females are the best teachers. And for all, there is a refining and restraining influence in the presence and coöperation of both classes in the common work. The advantages of this arrangement I have very thoroughly proved—especially as bearing on the one point of which I now speak. Years ago, I walked into a boy's school, connected with a church, and taught in its basement—where I found a complete uproar and mob. A teacher had in some way undertaken to compel a boy's submission, who found a protector in another teacher—till their loud quarrel overwhelmed the school completely, and I should be ashamed to record the things said and done, which I heard and saw myself. The origin I knew not. But the effect was indisputable. The teachers were both respectable gentlemen, but a hasty spirit stirred up strife—and there was no soft answer to turn away anger. The presence of the other sex would have rendered such a scene impossible. The influence of the common instruction of both is to instill a sense of propriety in the roughest—and to awaken and cultivate the very spirit of affection and the tenderness of manner and deportment of which I speak. And I have never seen the case of youthful hostility that affectionate treatment would not overcome, while some of the roughest specimens have brought out the purest and the most precious jewels I have ever had. To overcome evil by good, is the fundamental law of useful teaching. To persevere in the determination to do this, is the condition of its accomplishment. Do not charge me with dwelling too much upon this. Nothing can be forced in a Sunday-school. And all the other qualities being conceded, the whole success of the work, and the whole difference of success between two teachers in the work, will depend at, last on this simple quality of love in the heart, love in the manner, love in the voice, love in the judgment and estimation, love persevering through all obstacles and difficulties, until God has subdued the unruly and transformed the rebellious by the power of His own grace. This love will pray, and wait with patience, will forbear and plead with kindness. It will be seen and felt in all its manifestations. It will make a teacher exceedingly dear to the children—and a precious blessing to the school. How often do I catch the spark from such a face, and such a work, and bless God for the consolation which He imparts, from light and life that He has Himself kindled around me.

XI.

ONE qualification in our teachers remains
unnoticed, which must be deemed absolute and essential. It is punctuality.
Regularity of attendance—and accuracy of time. A shiftless, uncertain
Sunday-school teacher, sometimes present, sometimes absent—sometimes ready, generally late, is like a broken tooth, and a smoke
in the nose. No talents or qualifications besides, can compensate for the want of fidelity
in attendance or punctuality in time. Habits
of order are indispensable in this relation to
the comfort and to the success of the work.
The estimate of personal responsibility in this
engagement exhibited by a teacher—the seriousness with which the obligation is considered
—the facility with which it is neglected, or

some other call or obstacle is deemed an adequate excuse—are to be regarded as no less
than high moral traits, or radical moral defi-
ciencies. Always present, always ready, always
in time, are fundamental requisitions in a Sunday-school teacher. Nor can any excuse be
adequate or reasonable, which does not involve
some obstacle absolutely insuperable.   And
when absence is absolutely unavoidable, then
a fitting substitute should be sent in the place.
The Superintendent is most unjustly burdened, in the compulsion to hunt up impossible supplies, or to groan over vacancies which
can not be filled.

But suppose the agency thus far considered
to be adequate and real—and these conditions
all complied with—we are not then to forget
that this is one of those great works in which
the blessing of the Lord alone maketh rich.
As in the work of the appointed ministry, we
realize here in all our gains, and in all our disappointments, that without His power and
presence we can do nothing. The preparation
of the heart, and the answer of the tongue,

are both from Him. The forgetfulness and the
want of this Divine power, is an habitual
cause, I fear, of the failure of our hopes and
plans. The commanding, pervading idea and
feeling in the Sunday-school should be the
spirit and habit of prayer—sincere, earnest,
special prayer. The opening exercises of the
school should be in a spirit and manifestation
of real earnestness, in this one great purpose
of seeking the blessing of God. The whole
character and influence of these opening exercises of worship, should be such as to awaken
an interest in the minds of the whole school, a
consciousness of the solemnity of the occupation, a feeling of seriousness in the work to be
undertaken, and a real union of heart in the
prayer, and praise, and exhortation, to which
their attention is called. Every thing in the
manner of conducting this work becomes important. We are dealing with little minds,
and every little thing which may operate on
our relations to them is to be considered and
provided for. The teachers must be punctual,
and on the spot in time. The children must

be taught to assemble in seriousness and quietness. They must be in their places, in readiness for the opening worship of the school. To allow a habit of heedless, desultory coming is often to destroy completely the whole benefit anticipated from the gathering. We can not safely permit teachers and children to be absent from the worship, or to be tumbling in together, in a noisy disturbance of the tranquility and repose of its actual offering. This must never be considered a subordinate matter. We have but a short time for the whole work of the day. The loss of any part of it is important. And the idea can not be suffered, that the loss of the opening prayer is of less consequence than any subsequent portion of the privileges of the occasion. So necessary do I esteem this quiet and punctual commencement, that my hope of a blessing fails me if I can not obtain it. A few moments' silent thought and secret prayer by the teachers and children as they come to their places, is a blessed opening, and a most encouraging sight. It seems to say in its expressive form of utterance, " We are all here ready before the Lord, to hear all things that are commanded of Him." It inspires hopeful anticipations. The Lord the Spirit seems to be in the place, and the work of the day begins with the dew upon the grass. Often have I felt and enjoyed the encouragement thus divinely given. But when I see teachers and children gathering carelessly, wandering from place to place in the room— idly chatting with each other over some outside or worldly subject, a buzz of confusion, which, however natural to youth, is hostile to all the engagements of the hour and the place, my heart has sunk in sadness over the little prospect of a blessing on our toil.

The opening worship should be short, appropriate, and engaging. A hymn of praise adapted to the minds of children, animated and awakening—a few words of serious exhortation or address from the Superintendent to the teachers and children—a prayer adapted also to youthful minds, and expressed in such language and sentences as they can perfectly comprehend and enjoy—these may all occupy ten to fifteen minutes—in no case to be extended longer. This commencing work tests the skill and tact of the Superintendent. In it his manner and voice should be prompt and completely audible to all. His own real earnestness should command instant tranquility and attention. If he be truly qualified for his post, he will be heard, revered, and loved. Perfect order and silence should reign throughout while he is thus engaged; and the whole aspect and influence of the employment should indicate the presence of the Lord with His children, and the sincerity and spiritual character and habits of those who are seeking Him.

For this opening of the school, I by no means prefer a form of prayer, if the Superintendent be qualified to express with propriety and to edification, the wants and feelings of the children whom he represents. And of all the forms I have ever seen, I confess no one has appeared to me, in any sufficient degree, appropriate to the special demands of this occasion. There should be simplicity without trifling—true Scriptural sentiment in the plainest and

most intelligible terms—thoughts and wants
expressed such as children may truly feel—petitions calculated to lead their minds to an actual engagement in the worship. It is not a
prayer for the children. This may and ought
to be offered, indeed, by the teachers with all
their hearts. But this is a prayer of the children for themselves ; and, to be real and sincere, it must be such as they can understand
and appropriate without difficulty and in truth.
I dwell upon this because I esteem it a most
serious step in the work, either for good or
evil. Prayer is here, as everywhere, a real pe-
tition for blessings desired, and, because promised, expected. It is the real seeking of God's
own presence and blessing upon the work before them ; and it must, therefore, be a true
and living thing. I have been present in different schools, where the voice of the Superintendent did not reach the ears of many of the
children ; and where there was so much confusion and under-noise that his words could
not be fairly heard ; and where the language
was so mature and elevated that it was unin-

telligible and useless. Now if we are to consider this exercise as a priestly intercession for
others—then, so that the Being to whom it is
addressed understands it, the whole may be in
an unknown tongue to them. But we have no
such thought. It is a filial, united supplica-
tion of God's little ones to Him. It is the
cry of the lambs to the Great and Good Shepherd. If one speaks for them, they all speak,
and they have a right to an utterance which
they can make, and comprehend when made.
The positive, actual nature of real prayer must
not be forgotten. We can do nothing without
the Spirit of God. And we therefore combine
and agree to ask for His Spirit. The key to
the whole influence of the hour may be found
in this first commencement of the work.

This serious, earnest spirit should pervade
the whole occasion. We are dealing with im-
mortal beings upon everlasting concerns, and
the whole influence and feeling in the work
should be coincident with this commanding
thought. The general spirit of the place must
be earnest and solemn. There should be a

quietness which is the very result of this solemnity of feeling in the minds of all. It is dis-
mal to hear a Superintendent shouting for silence, and constantly ringing a miserable bell,
that seems itself to be the very sound and in-
dex of disgrace and indifference. So that the
voices engaged were really drawn out by earnestness in the occupation, I would rather hear
almost any amount of noise in the voices of
the children than this constant acknowledg-
ment of deficiency in the Superintendent.
What is wanting is an influence—the influence
of prayer—of real religious character and personal example—a pervading spirit of affectionate confidence, mutual and engaging, between
children and teachers and Superintendent.
And his presence and influence must be felt in
every portion of the work. Evils are to be
remedied by prevention. Difficulties are to be
anticipated. And a faithful and qualified Superintendent will carry round with him that
gentle and gracious authority which requires
no vehemence ; that personal character which
attracts and governs by attracting, rather than

10*

by any language of rebuke or displeasure. It is this spiritual, healthful atmosphere which is wanting first of all, in the agency of a Sunday school—the atmosphere of order, of love, of real earnestness in the Lord's work as here arranged. And though this is made up of details and elements, I first look at the combination in actual operation. The school thus described, is blessed in its whole character and results. When we enter it, and stand in it for a season however short, we see that there is a real earnestness and spirit of love at work, which could only come from God, and is the precious evidence that the Lord is there.

XII.

UR last view of the school in actual
operation, brings us at once to a point
which is of unsurpassed importance in
the general subject we are considering.
I mean the character and qualifications
of a suitable Superintendent. Everything in
the actual management of the work must depend upon him. His power must be supreme.
He is the executive officer of the little community; and however appointed, whether by
the pastors, or the Church, or the teachers, or .
be himself the pastor, he must be obeyed simply and implicitly in all the business of the
school in actual session. He has no time 'to
discuss questions there with any one. Not
even the authority which has constituted him
can be permitted there to interfere with the

work intrusted to him. He must designate and appoint the work and classes of the teachers. If teachers fail in efficiency or duty, the power of arresting the evil must be in his hands. And in the whole management and order of the operation in actual work, a clear and conceded supremacy must be in his person. Any other view of his rights and station, with the entire absence of means of mere physical control, would convert the school into a mob. And in selecting a superintendent, this whole view of power and responsibility must be clearly and fully met. You can not doubt, therefore, that the superintendent must be a person of very advanced and positive qualifications. And in proportion to the size of the school, will the demand for such qualifications be the more absolute and indispensable. Some of these qualifications, and by no means those of least consequence, will appear to be very external and secondary. Yet they must be had.

Inherent punctuality of nature, and invariable punctuality in habit, is indispensable. Never should one minute elapse from the ap-

pointed time of commencement, of division of
the work, or of the close. Punctuality in the
superintendent is punctuality in the root, for
the school. In every one else it must grow
from him. The absence of it there will break
up and wear out the most flourishing enterprise in this work. Order in arrangement and
in memory of his routine is equally indispensable. In no human relation is this habit of
more value and efficacy. The actual colloca-
tion of the classes—an eye to that which is
appropriate and suitable in inferior but not
unimportant circumstances, in the harmonious
adjustment of the whole, even in relation to
the beauty and propriety in the aspect of the
school—are here important facts. The first
look at a Sunday-school will, to an experienced eye, declare the character and adaptation of the superintendent. He should have
an adequate and prompt voice—that can be
heard by every one without effort or constraint
—that will be heard and understood at once,
from the simplicity and distinctness of its expression. Much of the happiness and success

of the school depends upon this. Teachers can not be confused with indistinct sounds, nor children bewildered with unintelligible commands. The superintendent's manner must be simple, prompt, calm, adequate to command attention, or he fails entirely. He must be a person of few words and peaceful habits. A perpetual haranguing—long, indefinite, and dilatory prayers—gangling and disjointed exhortations—habits of chattering and familiar interference with teachers or scholars, are more out of place in a Sunday-school, perhaps, than anywhere besides. Every thing must be real, actual, self-demonstrative, to command the attention or to win the confidence of children. These are all simple and external qualifications, but they are of immense consequence in the successful management of this work.

But there are much higher qualities which must be sought in a successful superintendent. He must be one of known and real Christian character—standing in the Church of God, both socially if possible, and personally surely, as a Christian of influence and acknowledged position. His office is to be one of personal influence entirely. It often is the fact, that one whose relations in the world are by no means exalted, may still be in the Church, from the known excellence of his character and fidelity of his walk, a person of distinguished influence and position. I have known many such, and some whose personal excellence and intelligence, though among the poor of this world, gave them a very commanding power in the Church. The superintendent of a Sunday-school must be known as a man of Christian holiness and fidelity—to whose counsel reference may be had in religious questions with confidence, and whose personal reputation at the head of his school will give reputation and authority to its teachers and scholars, as being engaged with him in such a work. He should be a man of earnest piety and prayer. He is to be the leader in a very important work for the Lord—a representative of the Church, and of the Head of the Church, in a very responsible relation, and should be one whose whole heart is in the labor in which he is to be engaged.

His personal influence is of vast consequence in its reflected power through all the week. If teachers must blush over the report of his short-comings in business or relative duty, or children must listen to his name mingled with expressions of derision or censure from others, it is impossible but that such facts must overthrow his whole power in his Sabbath work. He must be a person of quick and intelligent perceptions, so that he may become readily acquainted with the teachers, understand their characters and their peculiar wants—and be a kind and competent adviser to them in any questions in their work, or even in their personal condition, apart from this peculiar relation. He ought to be able to know the children personally, as far as possible, and at any rate to be able to discern the adaptation between the children and the teachers in their peculiar connections, on the successful management of which so much of the happiness and success of the school depends. He should be

a person of kind and friendly manners, win-
ning and retaining an affectionate confidence
in his sincerity and his real wish for the happiness of all who are here connected with him.
Perhaps in no other relation is this characteristic of greater consequence. And how much
comfort and pleasure a bland and conciliating
manner in the superintendent imparts to the
whole work of teaching and training in the
Sunday-school, many of our readers will be
able to testify from a variety of facts in their
own observation.

In addition to all these, a superintendent
must practically understand this work. The
Scriptures which are taught he must be able
to expound with propriety and usefulness in
the meetings of teachers, and to apply in
their principles, in short and useful exhortations, now and then addressed to the school.
The real purpose and method of the school
must be familiar to him; and if he be a
man of tact, of quickness, of intelligence, as
well as a mature and respected Christian, how
can he find a place of more usefulness or more

happiness than this ?   With such a head to
the school, how harmoniously and happily
every thing works !   And with entire mutual
confidence between the teachers, superintendent, and scholars, is there a place on earth of
greater happiness, or a work on earth of greater
delight, than the employment and exercise of
the Sunday-school ?   It becomes the abode of
peace and blessedness—a little heaven below.
The influence and atmosphere are all on the
Lord's side, and children grow up there with
all the tastes, habits, and advantages of which
I have spoken in earlier letters. I hope I shall
not be thought exacting or impracticable in my
views in this letter. I have had experience in
the past years, on both sides of this experiment, and speak in this, as on every other
point considered, just as I have been led to
think. It may be that such an utterance will
stir up superintendents as well as teachers to
an effort for constant improvement in their
own qualifications, and drive away the indolent thought, that all this is mere convenience
and not duty or necessity for them. Let us

realize the old proverb, that "whatever is worth doing, is worth doing well;" and with united hearts devote to this all-important work the best energies and the utmost industry which we can command in its prosecution.

XIII.

INCE I had the pleasure of writing my last, the Eleventh Anniversary of my Sunday-schools at St. George's has occurred, and furnishes a subject as an incident in our line of thought at this point. I have always counted much upon the influence of an interesting and well-arranged anniversary, as very important in a Sunday-school. And for this reason, I have been unwilling to merge my own local anniversary in any common meeting of children in school unions either of places or churches. The orderly influence of an appointed and regular anniversary as a point in arranging and completing the year's work and plans, is very valuable. It brings every part of the work up to a fixed settlement, and thus gives additional force

to the system and method of operation, and to
the consciousness and feeling of responsibility.
If well conducted, the exercises of an anniversary give solidity to the aspect of the school—
attract attention to it—tend to enlarge its
bounds by bringing in other children—give a
measure of satisfaction and contentment to the
scholars and teachers engaged—and make the
whole work appear as an actual and important
part of the congregation and church to which
the school belongs. I have never failed in carrying out this view in practical experiment for
more than thirty years past. And I am quite
satisfied, that no element in my management of
the Sunday-schools committed to me has been
more valuable, as an instrument of influence
upon others, either in the way of encouragement to other schools and teachers, or of enlargement of my own. The exercises of these
anniversaries have varied as our experience and
observation have advanced. For the first five
years of the period specified above, we were
merely accustomed to a few hymns, and an address or sermon, and felt unable to demand the

11*

foremost place for our children. So we placed
them in the gallery, and allowed the congregation to occupy the floor of the church. We
were few in numbers, and with but little comparative influence as an institution. When we
opened the church of the Epiphany twenty-
six years ago, we had made the Sunday-school
effort so fundamental 'there, that I felt able to
make a great advance. Then our anniversary
was made an occasion for itself, and we claimed
the floor of the church for the children, and
left the galleries to the congregation. This
plan of occupation I have never varied since.
There also I added, as a new feature, a donation of a book to every scholar, as an anniversary
token of affection and interest from the congregation. This also I have constantly maintained, considering it in no degree a reward,
and graduating the worth in no shape of proportion to supposed individual merit ; but having it bestowed and received as an expression
of interest and mutual remembrance. It delights me now to see in the houses of some of
my children quite a library of these anniver-

sary books, preserved with the utmost care, and valued as very precious remembrances of affection. They are little anchors of love and bonds of union, everywhere multiplied, which tend to hold these children fast to the Church in which they have been taught, and to the pastor around whom they have learned to cling. This is an expensive addition to the anniversary, but not more so than it is worth. I include it in my annual calculation of cost. And years of experiment have proved to me, that the whole cost of Sunday-school management on the most liberal scale, including question-books, Bibles, hymn-books, children's papers, libraries, and necessary printing, with the anniversary books added, may be brought within *two cents* a Sunday for each scholar. Surely the Christian Church can not ask for a more economical expenditure or more effective investment than this.

For six or seven years past we have added another important feature to our anniversary in our missionary arrangement. We used to be satisfied with a regular collection of money in the school, either weekly or monthly, for missionary purposes, and found it difficult to advance the effort or the interest beyond a very small amount. About the time just specified, Rev. Dr. Newton, my present excellent successor and brother at St. Paul's, Philadelphia, proposed and adopted a plan of organizing every class in his schools into a district mmissionary society, to collect its own funds, and report them with the amount presented at the anniversary of the school. The plan was beautiful in thought, and perfectly feasible and effective in operation. I could only congratulate my valued friend upon the conception, and cheerfully adopt it. I made it at once a part of my own anniversary proceedings. And it enlarged our missionary collections in the school the first year from $250 to $650, and it has now brought them up to more than $4,000, with no troublesome or burdensome effort. I have been delighted to see the same system carried out in multitudes of schools throughout the churches of our land. Every class is a missionary society, with its own name chosen by itself. Each one collects in its own way, and among its own social opportunities and relations, and by its own means. Accordingly, they must vary much in their results, as their circumstances, their interest, and their industry vary so entirely. Yet the poorer children and teachers are often not only the more liberal contributors in proportion to their means, but also often the largest in actual amount. These amounts are weekly and constantly gathered, and kept by an appointed treasurer for each class, and publicly presented at the anniversary in such shape as each adopts. Emblematic figures, baskets of flowers, or whatever token may occur to their own mind as most appropriate to the name adopted, are carried to the pastor, who presides at the anniversary, and the amount of each is separately announced. Then for the first time is it known to any one how much have been the missionary collections of the year. This new feature has vastly increased the interest of our anniversary occasions, and, as the results show, has added a great impetus to the growth and power of the school. We have, therefore, now incorporated this as an additional feature. In Dr. Newton's plan, the missionary collection has superseded the anniversary book, and the children are the only apparent givers. The view which I have taken of the anniversary books, made me wholly averse to taking from the congregation the privilege of giving to the children, and I have therefore maintained the united and reciprocal action—the children giving to the work of the Church of their own savings and collections—and the Church giving to the children, as their personal offering, a token of their interest and love. The proportion of the two is, that the Church give now to the children on this day not more than *one-tenth* of the amount which the children give to the Church. I do not think it necessary to go into the details of our school collections. They must always depend upon the earnestness, industry, and tact of the various teachers, scholars, and superintendent and pastor—and thus are an admirable school and exercise for all these gifts, and for their improvement, as the necessity becomes the mother of invention.

Our Eleventh Anniversary was held as usual on the afternoon of the Sunday after Easter, this year, the 15th of April. The galleries and vacant spaces beside the actual pews and aisles of the floor of the church, were given to the congregation, and were crowded long before our exercises began. The schools assembled at their rooms, and moved from thence to the church at 3 P. M. The pastor was in the pulpit to receive them. The organist played an accompaniment as they entered. They came in perfect order, and occupied the pews designated for them, each teacher preceding the class, and having a card indicating the aisle, the side of the aisle, and the number of the pews severally assigned. They entered the church in the following order : First, our Main or Church School. I. Female Bible-class, 1 teacher and 25 scholars. II. Female Bible-class, 1 teacher and 63 scholars. III. Male Bible-class, 1 teacher and 28 scholars. These may all be called adult classes. IV. The First

Infant-class, 1 teacher and 150 scholars. V. The Second Infant-class, 2 teachers and 309 scholars. VI. The Female Intermediate School, 32 teachers and 253 scholars. VII. The Male Intermediate School, 22 teachers and 189 scholars—making in our whole Church Sunday-school 63 teachers and officers, and 1,017 scholars. When all these were seated and arranged, in silence and without confusion, the English Mission-school entered, in the same orderly arrangement, preceded by their minister, Rev. Mr. Bolton. I. The Infant-school, 1 teacher and 150 scholars. II. The Female Bible-class, 1 teacher and 16 scholars. III. The Male Bible-class, 1 teacher and 10 scholars. IV. The Female School, 12 teachers and 96 scholars. V. The Male School, 14 teachers and 110 scholars—making 35 teachers and officers and 382 scholars. Following these, the German Mission-school entered, with their minister, Rev. Dr. Schramm, preceding them. I. The Male School, 4 teachers and 70 scholars. II. The Female School, 5 teachers and 61 scholars—making 9 teachers and 131 scholars. Our whole assemblage, therefore, amounted to 107 teachers, and 1,530 scholars. These are our parish Sunday-schools, exclusive of our parish week-day teaching work and numbers, which do not come up under this head, and which increase our whole number of teachers and children to 2,224. Our exercises were simple and familiar. The multitude of children united in their hymns in the fullest and finest manner. The Infant-schools and the German school each sung a separate hymn —the latter in their own tongue. The sermon was on the way to prosper in the Lord's work—from 2 Chronicles xxxi. 21, "In every work that he began in the service of God, he did it with all his heart, and prospered." These points were illustrated and enforced by facts and instances. 1. He *did it*. 2. He did it *with his heart*. 3. He did it with *all* his heart.—Thus he prospered. After the address, the missionary offerings were presented by messengers from successive classes. The sums varied from $2 up to $218, from different classes—amounting in the whole to $4,224.

12·

The Mission-school surprised and delighted me in this : the English school offering $163 75 ; the German school $18 50, and the Infant school $7 ; in all $189 25, from the children of the poor. It was most affecting to see four of these boys bearing on a platform a beautiful model of the Mission chapel, with a banner from the roof inscribed " Our Chapel,"—as the emblem of their gift and their school. After another hymn, the anniversary books were distributed through all the school, to every teacher and scholar—making about 1,600 volumes—expressive of the love and interest of the congregation. Two hours were occupied in all these exercises, and the crowd, unwearied, seemed unwilling even then to depart. The whole result was to create a deeper attachment in St. George's to our Sunday-school work, and to confirm my thoughts and convictions yet more completely in the conclusion long since adopted, of the unrivaled importance to a Sunday-school of a pleasant and effective anniversary.

XIV.

Y past letters have led to many inquiries and suggestions to me from friends and brethren in all directions, and upon all subjects in any way connected with our chosen theme. Many of these are so entirely theoretical in their character, that I can do little for them or with them. Important ecclesiastical questions and abstract schemes of doctrine and authority might be appended to these familiar letters by a mind more speculative or better taught than mine. But they do not present themselves in the line of my purpose, nor would the discussion of them appear to me profitable in this relation. My whole connection with Sunday-schools has been in their

common practical management. I have few
ideas and less taste to lead me in any way
wide of this simple line. But there is one
question repeatedly asked, the issue of which
is extremely practical to both sides involved,
viz. : What is the proper relation of the Sunday-school to the church.? Perhaps we are
bound in propriety of thought to look at this.
Yet I should wish to consider it in a very plain
and practical way. The term Church is really
so indefinite and multiform in its application,
that we feel ourselves encompassed by a cloud
whenever we employ it for any technical purpose. No single man uses it but in habitually
various connections, and no two men, perhaps,
give the same interpretation to it in their own
thoughts, when it is heard or employed. If
we take the Saviour's interpretation of His
Church,—Wherever two or three are gathered
together in His name He is also present with
them,—our Sunday-schools every where originate in the Church, and are a real embodiment
and accomplishing of the work of the Church,
and an exhibition of the Church at work in one of

the most important of its offices on earth—the feeding and guiding of the lambs of the Lord's flock. If we assume the title as describing the organized outward assembly of professed Christians in their concrete relation as a social body, then the Sunday-school may be considered as a separate part of the Christian work, and a distinct organization for its peculiar purpose of usefulness. In this view of the Church, it is certain Sunday-schools did not originate there. They were not created, nor for many years upheld, by any law or action of this body, wherever located. But this is equally true of the most of the works of Christian benevolence in the world. These have been habitually started by private and individual effort and agreement. The Sunday-schools of our country have generally originated in the personal, voluntary associations and labors of individual Christians ; often of Christians from various organized Churches, combining together as in a common cause, and for a common benefit. For many years the great majority of our schools were so sustained and so managed. And in the great

12*

efforts of our own time for extending and establishing Sunday-schools, the work is carried on by agencies wholly independent of any governing Church, and the schools established are far more generally the parents of Churches which grow from them, than the results of any Church management or action. It is this fact in the history of Sunday-schools which has given rise to the question proposed, and which perhaps has awakened and fostered in many cases a jealous spirit of independence, in fear of some relative action which may be undesirable and oppressive. Our Sunday-schools have been the results, on the one side, of human necessities perceived; and on the other, of the Christian spirit of benevolence and love divinely imparted. They grew up with the simple design and desire of direct usefulness to children neglected, and not from any plan of church-extension or organization as a scheme of work or power. They appeared to be the private property and enterprise of individual Christians. And when a community of persons who perhaps had done little or nothing individually to encourage and maintain them, claimed authority over them, a hesitation of submission was felt and expressed. by no means unnatural or, unreasonable.

But though there still remain many such schools, and such alone will be generally established among the scattered and neglected population of the poor, either in the cities or the remote settlements of the country, the actual connection of Sunday-schools with churches of every kind has at last become universal. Every church has its Sunday-school, and the most of Sunday-schools have an actual and inseparable relation to the Church in this connection. In this view, the term church has resolved itself in our use into the particular congregation of professing Christians in any constituted assembly for habitual worship, and under any name. And even then there is the distinction remaining, between that which this Church does through the voluntary agency of its individual members, and what it appoints in its corporate character. When we leave the Sunday-school of a particular Church to

arrange its own rules, and plans, and operations, in an association of its actual laborers—it
is as really a part of the work of that Church
as any other portion of its engagements and
duties for the Lord. Nor would it become
more really so, and generally not as profitably
so, if all its laws and plans were made part of
that church-action, in its technical and corporate
capacity. I am fond of the independence of
the Sunday-school. I desire to see it unham-
pered by external authority—and especially
unrestricted by laws and rules made by those
who do not work in it, and have no real experience of its operations or its needs. As a
practical fact, so far as I know, this independence has been the general rule of the operation. I have known no school over which any
Church professed to hold a dominance, or with
which the Church pretended any other interference than the desire and the obligation to
promote and sustain it with affectionate liberality and thoughtfulness. The feelings of the
Churches, or of Christians in their church-con-
connection and corporate character, have very

much changed in the history of this operation.
Sunday-schools were not regarded with favor
by Churches in their commencement. They
were often considered appendages of unnecessary cost, Sunday gatherings of children which
were a nuisance of inconvenience to older and
steady worshipers, and a new system of repub-
licanism in Christianity which threatened much
insubordination and possible conflict with hereditary and constituted power in the Church.

We who have worked long in the enterprise
well remember how many and great were our
difficulties in obtaining the aid, patronage, or
even the toleration of the elder Christians who
governed the Churches when we began. We
have lived to see a universal revolution in this
respect. The present Churches are, to a great
extent, manned and ruled by those who were
themselves educated in these schools. So that
now we rarely feel the want of patronage; but
rather fear the overaction of interest and control from the churches to which our schools
appertain. The aspect of the question of relation which now forces itself upon our minds

is not so much that of authority as that of
mutual duty ; not how much submission the
Sunday-school is to render to the Church, but
how much encouragement and aid the Church
is to render to the Sunday-school. In considering this question, however, there is a further
difficulty in the variety of incidental differences between the various local schemes of
church authority. I do not know that any
where, except it may be in some scattered cases,
it is the habit to settle interests of this description in a public meeting of church-members or
communicants, though these really constitute
the acknowledged Church in any given location
or in connection with any given edifice or house.
Such matters are left in the hands of a committee—or a session—or a vestry—as the different organic arrangement may be, who are
severally the representatives of the Church, and
authorized to act in its stead. The responsibility and the action of these appointed agents
are the responsibility and the action of the
Church. At any rate, so we must view it in
the considerations which may arise here. And

as the case stands before us, the question is, What is the duty of the Church, and what is the duty of the pastor, to the Sunday-school?

The duty of the Church, in discharging an immensely important part of its covenant obligation—and the duty of the pastor, in fulfilling an equally valuable and necessary portion of his appointed ministry—I will try to speak of both, as they have been spread before my mind and experience, in a simple and practical way. Questions of authority I need not discuss. I have never seen the Sunday-school which offered the least rebellion to a fostering Church, or a loving pastor—or a Sunday-school that did not delight in bringing all its fruits and gains, and in the utmost abundance possible, to the bosom of the Church for its enlargement, and to the heart of the pastor for his comfort. And I know no other relation on this side than affectionate gratitude for all the care and interest they see awakened for them.

XV

RELATION TO THE CHURCH.—DUTY OF THE CHURCH.—MIS-
SION SCHOOLS.

HEN we ask what are the relations of the Sunday-school to the Church, we place both of the parties involved in the question before our minds, in an actual and corporate existence. They seem to stand as individual responsible bodies, distinct and separate from each other, and to ask the question, What are we to do and to receive from each other in our reciprocal independent attitudes? And even this statement is not complete, for we find both these parties spoken of with entirely different interpretation and association. The Sunday-school may be an individual and local· school, and the Church a limited and local society of Christians of any name. Or the

Sunday-school may be the great, general enterprise, and the Church the whole corporate body of Christians of any particular denomination. I need not present even a more general view of the Church than this, though it would be quite possible. Now only the first of these statements of the proposition is the one of which I here speak. And as the term relations here simply means relative duties and obligations, we may so consider and speak of the subject. What, then, are the duties of a Church to the Sunday-school as an institution, within the limits of its operation and influence? Surely, first of all, to establish Sunday-schools to the utmost extent of their power. Every Church is bound, as a society or family of the Lord's people, to take the utmost care of the instruction and training of the youth belonging to them. The one great instrument in the salvation of men, is the Word of God. The earliest possible age in which this can be brought into effectual application to the souls of men, is the best period. The power is all of God, and the promise of

its exercise, to make our " children holy," is
also His. I must assume the fact, that there
is no other method or agency within our reach
so adequate or appropriate to this important
and desirable result, as Scriptural Sunday-
schools. I have illustrated this point perhaps
sufficiently in my previous letters. And I
must therefore assume the great obligation of
every Church to instruct and educate their
own children for Christ and heaven, to be iden-
tical with the obligation to maintain and establish Sunday-schools throughout the whole
field of their influence and responsibility. In
the purpose and social effort to attain this end,
there must be the largest scheme of work, and
the most liberal estimate and arrangement of
means to carry it out, within the control of the
particular Church. No religious or benevolent
object can be presented to a Church so commanding in importance, or so compensating in
results. Whatever, therefore, a Church can do
in any expenditure or provision for the Lord's
work upon earth, they are bound to do first
and most effectively for Sunday-schools within

their borders. I can not speak of this as secondary to any claim or call to be made upon them. The obligation to provide a decent and appropriate house for their own worship is no more imperative in their condition, than the obligation to make similar just and ample provision for the care and convenience of their Sunday-schools. The duty of supporting the preaching of the Gospel to the adults, and of maintaining the pastoral office for this purpose, is not more obligatory or needful than the duty of full and adequate provision for preaching the Gospel to the children in the appropriate arrangements of the Sunday-school. And whatever books or other means of accomplishing the work required are necessary, and are within the means and scale of the particular Churches, can not be withheld without unfaithfulness to the Lord, and injustice to those for whose salvation He has gathered His people as a Church and family for Himself. Whether this work be done by the Church as a legitimate body in any shape of common session, or whether it be done by the members of this body, acting in individual and voluntary association, does not seem to me to be a question of any consequence. In either case, the Church are doing the work required, and their own absolute duty, and in both cases they are doing it as the Church, and for the Church, which is equally and specially represented in each. I should deem it mere absolute duty in each case, and no more consider it a work of relative benevolence to others, than the analogous work of employing and supporting the ministry of the Gospel among themselves. The Sunday-school of the Church is a living part, and a most important part of that Church, and they must see that in the provisions which they make for it, all their children may be taught of the Lord.

But around every Church there is a field of local labor and usefulness among children who are neglected by others, and for whose soul no man cares. Here arises a local field for benevolence in this relation. These may be gathered into the nursery of the Church already established, and thus perhaps saved by the Lord's

blessing for ever, and made to carry the blessings of salvation to the families from which
they came. And our whole experience shows
us how appropriate and successful this class of
religious effort has been made in this relation
—and how richly and surely a Church so laboring and sowing gathers a harvest and wages
unto eternal life. Or this aggressive action
may be carried on in the establishment of mission or branch schools in neighboring and convenient localities. Then it becomes a benevolent agency of the most valuable character,
often raising whole neighborhoods to respecta-
bility and usefulness, and becoming the living
seed of other Churches to rise and flourish in
their turn, and to carry forward the blessed
work for others still beyond. All the refining
and exalting influences of which I have spoken
come into operation thus in new fields, and
exercise their power from new centers to per-
petuate and extend an agency of blessing to
mankind, unsurpassed in value or effect. But
this view, which has been thus far limited to
a locality, may be carried out to the full ex-

13*

tent of missionary extension of Sunday-schools through the limits of a nation or the world. I am persuaded that no benevolent action is more real and efficient to the utmost extent to which it can be spread abroad. And with the large and growing institutions which are engaged in this work in our country, there are abundant opportunities for the enlargement of the effort to the utmost extent to which any Church shall be found able to go. All the arguments and reasons which may be urged for the extension of the Gospel on the earth by any agency, will apply with equal force to this, and receive in addition all the peculiar obligations and promises which connect the interests and hopes of the Gospel so peculiarly and especially with the young.

This is the duty of the Church, and of every Church. And whether it be accomplished by this Church in its corporate character, or by its members in voluntary relations I am unconcerned, so that the work be done. I acknowledge my own taste to be to have as much as possible done in all the work of the Church

by individual Christians in cheerful and spontaneous action and labors of love—and as little
as possible required or left to the Church for
legislation and government in its organic character. I greatly prefer the living to the "dead
hands,"—and believe that the more the work
of doing good to men is committed to individual responsibility and elective association, the
more effective and living it will be. And when
the active aspect of this work comes into view,
and the teachers are considered by whom the
school or schools of any Church are to be conducted, whether they are designated by any
vote of that Church as a body, either mediately
or immediately, or agree in a voluntary union
of action for the purpose proposed—they are
the parts and members of the Church, and for
this purpose they are really the Church in action, and in action for the accomplishment of
a most important part of the duty of the
Church as the Lord's family and people on
the earth. They are gathered in His name, and
for His work, and with His presence, and especially as representatives of the particular

Church in which they work and to which they appertain. It seems to me a very worthless inquiry and mere barren technicality, whether this or that sequence of incidents has preceded and accompanies their work. The whole Church ought to teach—as resolved into a committee of the whole for such employment. They are all the messengers of that Son of Man who came to seek and to save the lost, and they are to follow His example and to walk in the line of His commandments and His purpose, in the fufillment of their duty as members of His family. If they will all be fruitful in the work, there will be no questions about mutual authority. Let them all continue to teach and preach the Lord Jesus Christ. Let the best, the wisest, the most experienced, give themselves to the all-important labor of saving others and leading the ignorant to the Saviour. In an active, earnest Church there will be no quarrels or questions. It is when Jeshurun waxes fat that he kicks. It is when men have settled on their lees that their love grows stale and their taste is corrupted. Then the lust of government creeps in, and while they will do nothing to help, they will be abundantly ready to do much to control and to impede. To my mind the Church is never more beautifully and really presented in its normal and living shape, than when engaged in the Lord's work and presence in feeding His lambs.

XVI.

THE duty of a Church to provide amply and liberally for the support of its Sunday-school, is a very practical and intelligible point. The various ability of Churches must be allowed to regulate the amount and degree of this provision, as of all the other obligations or benevolent expenditures of the Church. But we have a right to insist that this particular obligation shall not be made second or inferior to any other. I will not speak now of the minuter arrangements and provisions for conducting the school. But I must speak of the necessity of an adequate building, appropriately arranged. Much of the usefulness and success of the enterprise must depend upon this. It is impossible to maintain a school successfully without it.

When we began this work we knew but little of the conditions of success. We gathered our children in galleries of the churches, or, if permitted, which was rarely the the case, in the pews on the floor. The scattered children were beyond the reach of a Superintendent's voice, and without the means of any sympathy with each other in a common work. The teachers were placed in such awkward personal relations to the children that no successful impression could be made, and no direct personal instruction given. The whole attempt was an inevitable failure, and the cause suffered much by it. A second stage in our operations, and a great advance, as it was esteemed at the time, was to dig out a better cellar for the church, and pack our children there. Here we fought with damp, and cold, and fetid atmosphere, till our universal experience convinced us that though the Gospel might flourish in involuntary dungeons and catacombs, a chosen cellar for it was no adequate or appropriate place. I have occupied such a cellar until the floor fell down beneath our feet in its quick but natural decay. Our Churches have been rapidly getting their schools out of damp cellars, and erecting suitable and appropriate buildings expressly for their use. And much of our manifest gain and improvement are arising from this one source. I hardly see a new church now erected in this city which consigns its schools to the tombs, and compels its best agents to complain, "*clamavi e profundis,*" in the prosecution of their important work. Comfort and convenience in arrangement, I am thankful to say, habitually distinguish our more modern preparations. To classify the children, to bring them together as a collection of little congregations, in one audience, to place them in direct and easy communication and sympathy with their teachers, to give them the opportunity of familiar instruction without noise or effort—we must have a compact, accessible, and well ventilated room, with seats and construction expressly prepared for the purpose. It must be open, airy, light, and attractive, so that the influence shall be in all respects exhilarating and encouraging. What

I should like to have for such a work I have never yet seen, for I have never yet seen a Church willing to make the effort, or informed enough to cherish the purpose, for such provisions as I have felt the cause deserved. The best I have ever attained, is to make, in the best way I could, the same room answer for a Sunday-school and for the weekly meetings of the adult congregation, a scheme involving very great, and, in some respects, insuperable difficulties. Could I have the least influence with the Churches, I would entreat them to make distinct, adequate, and appropriate accommodations for their Sunday-schools, entirely independent of any other use. Our congregations often complain of the want of such arrangements for their own united worship, and justly enough, for the problem of ecclesiastical architects seems often to be how to make the occupants of their buildings most uncomfortable. But the difficulty becomes just so much the greater, when the interests and habits of children are concerned, from their greater sensibility to material comforts, and their less power of

14

calculation and self-control. And if a Church find that they must make themselves *comfortable* to be *good*, we say, with so much more force of truth, so must they also provide for the children of the Church yet more abundantly.

The consideration of this material point leads me to speak of the provision to be made for mission schools. This is a new branch in our work, which has grown up lately and rapidly, and with much encouragement. Our Churches of all kinds are generally composed of self-supporting and comparatively respectable families. Indeed, the Christian and Church influence will be habitually to make them so, in the result. The elevating and refining power of the Gospel in the social and personal relations of men, is one of the wonders of its constant operation. And wherever we begin our work for the Lord, with whatever class or character of low and neglected population, the result is always the same. We lift the portion on whom we particularly operate, out of their former condition, and leave still behind the

mass from which they have been taken—just
as destitute and as poor as before.   In our
mission schools, therefore, there will always be
a calculation of a Church and congregation
that will grow out of them. All their relations
local and social, will undergo a distinct trans-
formation, and their associations and anticipations will be of a new and far superior stamp.
Of these mission efforts in our cities and towns
two separate classes present themselves.   The
purpose to constitute an actual, self-supporting
Church is one.   This is a frequent, and, if well-
managed, a successful experiment.   A Sunday-
school in a poor neighborhood will grow into
such an establishment in a few years ; and, if
fairly encouraged, will soon entirely take care
of itself. A congregation of thriving and prosperous people, even in small lines of earthly
business, will accrue around it, and a Church
of permanent character and influence take its
place.

Many such instances will occur to the minds
of those who are familiar with this subject.
But the unquickened mass behind remains the

same. And there needs, therefore, besides, a constant mission work which shall be considered as such alone :—a work which shall be for the poor—the poorest—and shall conduct them individually up to a higher stand, but shall not be expected to take a higher stand itself. These two efforts can never be mingled. There is in our country a pride and jealousy among the poor, which is one of the hardest elements to govern or propitiate. If a family of their own number and personal acquaintance, by employment and sobriety are elevated in their condition and comforts of living, and are seen in their congregation with new clothing and better appearance, the effect almost certainly is to drive back the others who have not so succeeded. The consciousness of their own appearance and poverty mortifies them so much the more in the comparison. They object to coming when others around them look so much better and dress so much more nicely than they. This spirit we have constantly to encounter. And, therefore, my experience leads me to say that we can never confound these two missionary efforts. We are to start one with the intention of raising it as an effort—and the other with the opposite plan, of keeping it down as a scheme, though by it we may and must raise the individuals connected with it. Of the two, this latter is peculiarly the missionary work. The other might be more justly called an enterprise or investment—profitable, indeed, in the highest degree. But this is a work for the poor, and among the poor, and the poor alone. A more blessed and important work can hardly be conceived. The poverty of our country is peculiar. No European rules or experiments answer any purpose as an example or precedent for us. In all those there is a fundamental distinction of classes acknowledged on both sides. Poverty there, to a great degree, may be contented poverty, and willing to be relieved as poverty. Here there is no social point so low that the man and the boy does not hear from others of the oppressions and the possibilities of their condition. Something better, something higher, is for ever in the view, and the subject of discussion. And the characteristic of American poverty is everywhere discontented poverty, aspiring poverty, and must be dealt with as such. We have, therefore, to arrange our outside Sunday-school efforts with these facts in our constant view, and wisely plan for the accomplishment of the ends we propose, with the clear and distinct consideration of them. This point I must endeavor to illustrate more particularly.

XVII.

HE subject of mission-schools, of which I spoke in my last, has assumed, for a few past years, new and enlarged importance. We formerly held them with no distinct individual design connected with them. We collected them and taught them in our public school-houses, or in any convenient attainable place. The whole idea was immediate present instruction to the children, with no view of any definite result into which the operations might grow. Many of these schools, accordingly, were merely temporary efforts, and passed soon and entirely away. The benefits conferred by them upon individual children might be real and abiding. The solid and substantial benefit to the community was not seen. Our later habit has been to set up these mission-schools with the distinct idea of some permanent influence and organization, looking in some shape to the establishment of a Church of some kind that will grow out of it. So that our Sunday-schools have become more and more the germs of living and permanent Churches—and thus have gained an increasing aspect of abiding usefulness in the community. The character and proportion of our poor population have very much changed during the process of this effort. I shall not trouble myself with attempted accuracy of statistical statements in this connection. But all who are actively engaged among the poor will realize the fact that American poor people are becoming remarkably few, while the amount of foreign pauperism is immense. This is a population with no plans nor hopes. It floats to our shores, and settles, for the time, wherever it can, mainly in our cities—content to have a shelter for a season, and with no definite anticipations of any permanent result. They are a very difficult population to help or benefit. Whatever is done for them is like salting a running stream. It must be constantly repeated, carried out on a permanent system, or it is useless. This is the class among whom our mission-schools are mainly established. The old meeting of rich and poor together in our earlier and smaller Sunday-school work, has yielded very much to this new aspect of affairs. The poor of whom I now speak can hardly be induced to come to our actual Church-schools, and mingle on an equal ground with other children. This view is realized perhaps more completely in this city than elsewhere. Here it must be met and calculated upon continually.

In such circumstances I will illustrate a plan by a particular history. Perhaps six years since, we found the difficulty of which I speak pressing us in St. George's, and determined in some way to meet it. We hired a room in the midst of our poorest neighboring population, and opened a mission-school. We scoured the neighborhood for children and teachers, and found great willingness on the

part of both to come in. We soon collected a
school of two hundred children, and acquired
the labor of faithful teachers of different de-
nominations. It was the first effort of the
kind in our region of the city. Not long after
our Baptist friends, some of whom had engaged
with us, believed that the whole work would
prosper more in a separate and independent
action, took possession of another room, and
soon had a nice building erected for them
about two blocks from us, by a very liberal
gentleman of their Church, since deceased—
in which they are still successfully at work.
Soon after, another neighboring Episcopal
Church pursued the same course, and it has
resulted in the erection of a neat and attractive chapel, a little more distant, which promises to be an independent and self-sustaining
Church. Not long after our Presbyterian
neighbors gathered another school of the same
description a few blocks off in another direction, which has also flourished, though not
yet in the erection of another building. In
the meantime our mission-school grew and en-

larged itself continually, and seemed benefited
by the extending of the spirit and feeling in
the neighborhood. We had just so much enlarged the market and the supply. And now
we found ourselves with so large a portion of
German children, to whom English teaching
was of no avail, that we separated them also,
to another room and place, for practical instruction in their tongue. Thus the whole
effort extended itself until the summer of
1858, when we determined to erect an adequate
chapel for ourselves. The children of the
Church Sunday-school undertook to pay for
the building, if the Church would pay for the
lots. And we commenced in that autumn,
and finished our chapel in the autumn of
1859 ; an edifice of eighty-five feet by fifty-
two, with a tower and bell—finished completely with organ and every proper appendage
to the most decorous worship, and with abundant rooms for schools and teaching, at a cost
for the building and furniture, of seventeen
thousand dollars, which was to be paid by the
collections and efforts of the Sunday-school

children. This beautiful building was fully occupied in September, 1859, and has been a completely successful and happy experiment. It accommodated our German and English schools and congregations in the two stories, with abundant room at the time of its occupation. But they have already outgrown the place, and we must now take measures for the separate accommodation of the Germans again. I consider this work so practical and so exemplary as an experiment of mission-school work, that I shall describe its details more minutely.

Its plan is free worship for the poor. It has no collections from them for the expenses of the chapel, though they have solicited the privilege of contributing, in their degree, to outside objects of benevolence. It is not intended to grow into a self-supporting Church —or in any improving aspect of it to shut out at any time the poorest of the poor from the worship and instruction which it offers. Every thing is done to make them all feel at home, and entitled to all the blessings which it offers to them all. An American clergyman is the pastor of the English-speaking flock, and a German clergyman is the pastor of the Germans. The sexton has a residence for his family in the building, and thus has opportunity for entire charge and protection of the property. On every Sunday, at 9 A. M., the English and German schools both assemble in their different rooms—the one averaging three hundred and eighty, and the other one hundred and forty attendants. At $10\frac{1}{2}$ A. M. there is public English worship in the Chapel, which seats about eight hundred. At $1\frac{1}{2}$ P. M. there is public German worship in the same chapel. At $3\frac{1}{2}$ P. M. there is again public English worship in the chapel. Thus the whole Sabbath is occupied with a busy stirring work for the poor. The teachers are, perhaps, more interested in the work than in most of our Church-schools, and have labored with a self-denial and devotion exceedingly encouraging and satisfactory. The Lord has smiled upon the effort so abundantly, that, as I have remarked, we are already crowded, and are compelled to look to another enlargement.

In the week there is a daily English school of one hundred and thirty children. There is a reading-room for men and boys open every evening from 6 to 9 o'clock, comfortably furnished, and provided with an increasing library, and papers and magazines. There is an evening lecture for the English congregation on every Tuesday evening, and a prayer-meeting every Thursday evening. There is also a lecture for the German congregation every Friday evening. And a sewing-school for girls of both on every Saturday morning. Thus the whole time is occupied, and the work is constantly going on. The English pastor has his study and office in the chapel, and there attends to the wants and calls of the people of his charge. There are now two hundred and twenty-one English and seventy-eight German families in actual connection with the mission, with one hundred and thirty-four communicants in the English, and thirty-six in the German congregation. The Lord has graciously blessed the operation in a very remarkable degree ; and every visit to it in any

of its departments and details only enlarges
and impresses my view of its important and
invaluable influence. Perhaps this is as successful an experiment of a mission-school as
has yet been made ; and I know no point in
which it has failed or disappointed our just
expectations. The cost of managing it in all
its details, will be within four thousand dollars
a year. Already it has blessed many souls
with salvation. It has elevated and improved
the whole neighborhood around it. It has exceedingly attached the poor to its privileges,
and has become a very popular effort both in
the congregation of our Church, and among
the poor who enjoy it. I have given its details in this connection as an illustration of
what may be done by voluntary effort in this
work, and as an encouragement to the toil of
other laborers in the cause.

XVIII.

THE duty of the Church to Sunday-schools is by no means exhausted, in the efforts of individual and separate congregations. The work has now grown to a great cause in the land and in the world. And the whole Church has to consider it as an inseparable institution in the effort of edifying and carrying on the Lord's work among men. This relation is probably a lasting and final one. Its local and demonstrated influence and value in connection with individual congregations, have displayed clearly to view its importance as a missionary and propagative arrangement in every outlying field of earth. What is it, after all—but the Church and Gospel for children ?   It is a divine arrangement for Christian education ; for bringing the Gospel in direct and appropriate application to youthful minds.   It will, therefore, present itself as the habitual and anticipated instrument for the religious instruction and welfare of the youth in every land, under its faithful employment in Christian wisdom and skill.   In our land the Sunday-school effort assumes a very peculiar importance as a sure scheme for the religious education of our children.   And when we estimate properly the relation of this to adult religion, we must say still further, it is the most hopeful scheme for the religious welfare of the nation.   Family religious teaching, precious and important as it is, can be calculated upon only in a very small comparative portion of our population.   Myriads of families are among us, rich and poor, where it would be vain to hope that the least regard to the religious instruction of the children would be found.   And, as I have already shown, no family religious teaching can accomplish all the benefits which Sunday-school in-

struction is adapted to confer.   Public secular
education can never be calculated upon as in
the least degree supplying the want.   The con-
test even for the remotest form of religious ac-
knowledgement and observance in our public
schools, is more and more unpromising as time
goes on.   The defense which is made for any
religious element in it, is at this time owing
almost wholly to the influence of our Sunday-
schools.   And the continuance and still more
the enlargement of this element in public education, will only flow from the same source.
So far, therefore, will our public schools be
from supplying the great want of religious
teaching, that they will not be able to hold
their own ground in this relation, but as an adjunct to the still more distinct and decided operation of the Sunday-school.   It is most true
in this respect that the Sabbath sanctifies the
week.   Take away the influence of our Sunday-school work as now carried on, and I apprehend the controversy for any religious aspect
in our weekly public schools would be much
more readily settled.   Whatever, therefore, is

the importance of the religious education of
the young, must be the estimate of the value
and necessity of the universal establishment
and maintenance of Sunday-schools. And,
as we survey the immense field which our
country presents in limits of population and
settlement, constantly enlarging, we see myriads of youth and children, who are apparently to be taught the Word of God, and to
be made partakers of the salvation which it
reveals, only in the extension and support of
the Sunday-school cause as widely as it can be
carried out.

This displays the duty of the Church in its
most general aspect to the nation in which it
is established. The Christian Church in this
country is to sustain the responsibility of extending the Gospel through the millions of our
increasing population. Their instrument for
this work, as manifestly laid upon them by a
gracious Providence, is the Sunday-school enterprise. The principles and details already
laid down, come into direct application to this
larger field. Just the obligation which impels

a single congregation to provide for the missionary instruction of the poor and ignorant in its neighboring localities, must lead the whole body of Christians to employ the same thoroughly tried instrument for an extended evangelizing of the young in the scattered and outlying districts of our immense territory. This becomes, truly and effectually, a missionary work of the most blessed and effective value. There is hardly a settlement in the land, in which a Sunday-school may not be established. The reports of Sunday-school missionaries laboring in our distant regions, and the experience of many individual Christian men and women in their personal efforts, have demonstrated the facility with which this work may be accomplished. Barns and sheds, schoolhouses and private dwellings, have furnished a temporary but real abode for schools collected from scattered neighborhoods where but few, and sometimes but a single real Christian could be found to undertake and carry on the work. Children have gathered from the cottages of the poor in the woods and mountains with delight—walking often miles to reach the humble but attractive spot where they might learn what God's dear Son had done for them. The reports of this work present some of the most affecting and encouraging details which are to be found in Christian history, of the eagerness with which the poor and banished have sought the privileges thus offered, and the grace and bounty with which God has been pleased to bless them. The instruments in such relations are often but partially qualified. Men and women cheerfully undertake the work of teaching to whom the Word of God has yet never been made the power of the Spirit for their own conversion. And though I have laid down as a principle the absolute necessity for religious character and experience, as quali-fications for Sunday-school teachers—we can not apply this principle as a rule of exclusion in these scattered and missionary fields. Rather we must welcome all to come, to teach and study together. For in such cases, it is more frequently a mutual study than a relative in-struction in the Word of God. All that has

been said of the influence and results of mission-schools, in more accessible localities, is
equally applicable to these extended missionary
efforts. Many Churches have risen from the
bosom of these mission-schools—in the most
remote sections of our land. A young man of
my acquaintance, a mere youth, was thrown
into a settlement of the Far West, and commenced, alone, a Sunday-school. His school
gathered increasing numbers from the wilderness around him, till parents and children all
collected, made the necessity for a permanent
house of worship. With the utmost effort
among his friends, he gathered means to build
his little temple in the woods. Soon his adult
congregation filled it up—and one hundred and
forty children were taught upon benches under
the trees, because there was no room for the
Sunday-school in the church. He was soon
enabled to enlarge his building, and a respectable, orderly, religious establishment has grown
out of it. This is but a specimen of hundreds
of similar history.

In what cause can the Christian Church ex-

pend its funds, or extend its sympathies, more
wisely and effectually ?   To provide adequate
books and means of teaching for a country like
ours must demand a large outlay of money and
effort.   But no money can be expended more
economically, or more effectually, for the welfare of our country or the salvation of our people.   The work will demand united effort.
But the means for this have been abundantly
prepared by the same merciful Providence that
has awakened and organized the scheme which
demands them.   The American Sunday-school
Union is a noble instrument for carrying the
Gospel to the children of our wide-spread
country, ready with its machinery and its
abundant material—asking only the zeal and
coöperation of the Churches, to extend a hun-
dred-fold the blessed influence which it is
already exerting in our nation.   Almost every
organized body of Christians has a union or
society of its own, for a kindred purpose,
mingling its own peculiarities of faith in a
prismatic division of labor, with the pure ray
of divine and simple salvation in the crucified

and exalted Son of God. I do not mean to contend with either or any of them. I would rather urge and encourage them all. But let the Church and the Churches arise and build —by either instrument, by both, by all—that we may serve and save our generation, according to the will of God. Let no demand for aid in the work be rejected from indifference to the object. Let the whole earnestness of Christian love and conviction be directed to this great purpose and its blessed results. Let the American Church determine that the children of America shall everywhere be taught the religion of their fathers, and that none shall be so scattered abroad that the missionary influence and effort of the Gospel shall not reach them. Let Christians delight to survey the field, the appropriateness of the instrument, the adaptation of the work to bless youth abroad, and then consecrate their liberality, sympathies, labors, and prayers, in a generous arrangement and measure, to the prosperous extension of the Sunday-school enterprise, in all its details of blessing, to the utmost borders of our country.

XIX.

O refer to the duties and obligations of the Church in relation to Sunday-schools, either as a local instrument or as a general cause, compels the consideration of another very important department of this great subject. You will surely anticipate me, in suggesting the relations and obligations of the ministry. The local Church, without its pastor, is but a body in action without its head. And the whole Church of the Lord, separated from the leading and coöperation of its appointed ministry, in any scheme of effort, must always be feeble and imperfect. I shall not diverge into any consideration of the powers of the ministry, or touch upon the various views which different

16

bodies of Christians may cherish in regard to the official relation of the ministry to the Church. None will deny the general principle, that the pastoral office, in all its relations, is designed to be leading, exemplary, and helpful to the Church of God, in the fulfillment of its great appointed work of glorifying Jesus in the publication and establishment of His Gospel among men. The description which the Holy Spirit gives us of this relation is adequate and complete—"When He ascended up on high, He led captivity captive, and gave gifts unto men. And he gave, some apostles; and some, prophets; and some, evangelists; and some, pastors and teachers; for the perfecting of the saints, for the work of the ministry, for the edifying of the body of Christ."—Eph. iv. 8. This is the ministry in its active and appropriate operation; and whatever becomes the obligation and duty of the Church, in extending the knowledge of the Saviour's love, must be of necessity the coördinate obligation and duty of the ministry, in its relation as the earthly, but Divinely-appointed guide and helper of the Church, in the great work of its earthly station and responsibility. All the suggestions which have been made, therefore, of the duty of the Church in this great and varied Sunday-school work, become yet more effective and appropriate in application to the ministry, raised up for the very purpose of leading on the Church to usefulness and triumph.

If we take our last most general view of the subject, I should ask my brethren in the ministry to consider the importance of their responsibility in relation to this. They can never be uninterested in a scheme of influence and labor of any kind which is to result, under the Divine blessing, in the salvation of many souls. The actual results of the Sunday-school work in the course of its past history should be a subject of study and earnest consideration. I can not doubt that its influence in arresting the power of imported evil, and resulting propagation of crime, in our country, has been a chief element in the peace of the nation, and a power whose extent it would be impossible for us to trace completely. The torrent of youthful debasement and immorality, of cultivated ignorance and infidelity, which has poured in upon us for these many years, has found no agent of resistance or removal equal to this. Millions of children of the poor would have grown to maturity in hopeless depravity, during the last twenty-five years of heavy immigration of the toiling population of the European world upon our scattered people, but for the blessed efforts of our Sunday-schools. A gracious Providence has appeared to prepare our great religious institutions, all of which find their best and 'most effective contact with the people through the Sunday-school, as a special depository of Divine agency and power for the safety and welfare of our land at this very time. The Bibles, and tracts, and books which are made ready for effective usefulness, are carried by our Sunday-schools directly to the very minds, which are taught to value them, and made able to read them to advantage. No intelligent observer can go through the Sunday-schools of this nation, including three millions of children or more, without discovering that more than one-half are of a parentage and national extraction which would have doomed them to ignorance and left them to perish in debasement and neglect. The children themselves habitually rejoice in these privileges. They breathe a free air with delight. They love to be taught the Word of God, and to learn the voice of prayer and praise. Within the last twenty-four hours, while I write, one of my teachers has reported to me a visit to a poor German Jewish family in our neighborhood. The father, who is a butcher, refused to hear or receive any tract or invitation to the school or church, and the teacher departed. A little boy, his son, who was sitting by, followed the teacher to the next house, and begged him to take him to the Sunday-school. The father consented to the boy's wish, and another child of ignorance will, by God's blessing, be reclaimed and taught His Word. This same day another teacher has given me an account of a group of Roman Catholic children, whom

16*

she had been teaching. They were happy and improving, learning their Bible stories and hymns with joy. They were, however, removed against their earnest desire, and placed at Popish schools. Some **had** been so unhappy that they had returned. But they had been taught nothing in their absence but some of the superstitions and errors of their corrupt faith, in which they felt no interest. There are millions of such children in our land, for whom there is no other available or effective instrument of instruction and improvement but the Sunday-school. This blessed instrument now meets them in every town and city, and even far off in their rovings and settlements in the wilderness. It becomes to them the present living agent of Gospel teaching and Scriptural truth. It is intelligible, immediate, and accessible to them all. What can supply its place? What could fulfill its work if left by it undone?

How incalculably blessed and useful is this work to these myriads of the poor and the neglected! How certain is its influence for the

welfare of our nation and the prosperity of the
Church of God among us ! I can not but appeal to the ministry of the Churches to take
hold of it, and encourage it, and carry it forward to a successful triumph. By whatever
agency of propagation they may prefer to ·act,
is it not their highest interest and duty to
work by it, and with it, for the great purpose
of general evangelization for which it is designed, and in which it has been so successful ?
Surely the Church never can go forward adequately in this work, unless the ministry take
the lead. Their opinion, their words of encouragement and appeal, their personal and
pastoral influence, given in their appropriate
measure to the effort, insure its success—and
encourage the judgments and the liberal action
of the Churches committed to them in this relation. They sow the seeds of Divine benevolence in a multitude of minds, which may
bring forth much and long-continued fruit,
abounding to the Saviour's glory in this relation. I would by no means prescribe the
mode of their action. Whether they shall

open their pulpits to appointed agents, for the special pleading of the cause, or choose themselves to be the advocates of a cause in which their own minds and hearts have become enlisted ;—whether they shall make public stated or occasional collections for the promotion of this cause in the congregation, or open the way by personal recommendations, for private and individual appeals, are points of machinery and discipline which must be left entirely to their own judgment and choice. I only plead for their interest in the cause itself, and their earnest coöperation to extend it. I beg them to give their minds and hearts to this work, as a great national and evangelical work, beyond the bounds of their own congregations, and the limits of their own neighborhood ;—to consider whether there is any other comparable instrument to bless the children of the nation, to forestall the power of evil, and to direct the little streams of the water of life to the very roots of the young and thriving plants of the future orchards of the land. The thought reminds me of a beautiful fact which I witnessed in the luxuriant orange gardens of Jaffa. A large stream of water issued from a cistern in a yard inclosed with a high wall. "A fountain sealed, a spring shut up, a garden inclosed." (Song iv. 12.) I followed it as it branched off, amidst the orange, citron, and lemon trees which covered many acres around. It ran in diverging streams, in multiplied channels. Each one ended at last where a single man was tending it with his bare foot, and directing it to the root of every single tree in succession. The skill with which he managed it was beautiful. The efficacy of the application was most remarkable. The manageable nature of the power of life, as he applied it, was very affecting. How like Moses' description, Deut. xi. 10: "Where thou sowest thy seed, and waterest it with thy foot, as a garden of herbs!" How like the actual Divine arrangements for bringing the water of life to individual souls! How precisely like the Sunday-school effort for this purpose above all other arrangements besides! How many of my brethren are like the man at the wheel of

the cistern, in the garden inclosed, commanding a settled power in a flourishing and established Church. Oh, let them send out the
stream beyond the walls! Fresh, growing
trees, promising future fruit, are standing
there in crowds. Agents of fidelity and skill
are standing also there, waiting to direct the
living water to every single plant, hidden in
the multitude. The life-giving stream will
bestow its joys and blessings upon millions,
from whom future fruit in grace and glory
shall be gathered. The Great Head of the
living Church will find the joy and the glory
His as He makes His gracious visits to His
heavenly garden in the earth. They may
themselves also partake of the joy and the
glory in personal visits to the results of their
work. "I went down into the garden of nuts,
to see the fruits of the valley; to see whether
the vine flourished, and the pomegranates
budded." They may also find the testimony
true: "Or ever I was aware, my soul set me
on the chariots of a willing people." (Song
vi. 12.) No labor can be more surely remu-

nerative to them—none more honorable to the Lord whom they serve. Dear brethren, let our hearts and minds be these "chariots of Amminadib," in this blessed work ; let us actively send forth our streams of blessing through all the land ; and "sow our seed beside all waters." It will be a glorious work for Christ. It will be a blessed work for perishing souls. It will be a joyful work for us. It will be a happy work for our nation. It will be a crown for our eternity.

XX.

THE reciprocal relations between the Sunday-school and the Church have presented us several topics for consideration. Not the least important of these is the one which occupied my last—the proper relations of the ministry to the Sunday-school. The extended view which we took in the last letter, is of vast consequence, The influence of the Christian ministry in this country is very great. It is not merely the influence of official position, which maintains its hereditary hold among us, notwithstanding all the modern attempts to undermine and destroy it among the multitude of our people. But it is also the far greater influence of demonstrated ability, education, purity of character, earnestness, and prudence, in the great body of the ministers of all the Churches, transmitted and perpetuated as the abiding characteristics of the American Church. I am fully convinced no nation shows a ministry more independent, more exemplary, or more respected among the people for whom they labor. To gain their influence, therefore, in any walk of benevolent effort, is of great consequence to its power and success. Our Churches will not be led to that enlarged and earnest plan of thought and action in the Sunday-school cause which its importance demands, unless the ministry of the Churches assume their place in leading on the undertaking, to the utmost of their ability to excite and maintain it. For this reason, I am earnestly desirous to awaken and encourage, if I could have power to do so, the eager and persevering coöperation of the ministry in the great general cause, as already laid out. But I am persuaded this will only grow as the fruit of a more direct and personal connection with the work, in their separate, individual fields of labor. The neglect of the local schools of their own Churches

17

can produce no earnestness or willingness for a
united effort to spread this system and agency
of blessings abroad for the benefit of others
unseen and unknown.

It would seem almost derogatory to the
character, and suspicious of the sincerity, of a
minister of the Gospel, to urge him to a pastoral care of his own Sunday-school, or to ask
whether such a pastoral care is really given.
And yet from the multiplied information I have
received, I am persuaded the subject, in its most
local relation, has received far less attention
than its importance claims. Doubtless there
are cases in which the pressure of a large city
Church, with all its various interests and calls,
may seem to consume all the energies and time
of a pastor, and furnish the apparently adequate excuse for inattention to the Sunday-
school. But I apprehend the difficulty is not
found more habitually in our large city
Churches than in others of a much more limited character. Not long since, I was visiting
in a beautiful country village, extremely compact, where every family could hear their

church-bell—and the perfect quietness of the
Sabbath morning seemed to woo the kindest
pastoral attention to every class of the people.
A beautiful little church edifice was there—a
congregation perhaps of two hundred people—
and a struggling Sunday-school of sixty or
seventy children, maintained by a few youthful
Christians of both sexes. The answers to my
questions presented the fact, that for months
together, the pastor, who lived within the hearing of the very singing of the children, did not
enter the school, paid no personal attention to
its condition or its wants, and in no way of
apparent personal effort attempted to promote
its success. And yet this minister was a religious and exemplary man, and in his conversation seemed alive to the reality and importance
of his own work, and the religious needs of his
people. It was surely an unaccountable neglect. But it could be paralleled by hundreds
of cases. And when, in this case, the complaint was made to me of the smallness of the
salary, of the indifference of the people, of the
coldness of their religious state, etc., it was

only astonishing to me that the good man was incompetent to see the root of the whole difficulty in himself. If such a man would take hold of his work personally, earnestly, and give himself to it, and, most of all, to this most important part of it, he would find his wilderness to blossom as the rose. "Like priest, like people," will be found a governing rule in all these relations.

Do you ask me what I would have such a man to do? I answer without hesitation, Take the personal charge and superintendence of his own Sunday-school. Give his mind, and time, and presence, and actual labor to the work of saving and teaching the children of his flock. What else should he do? His whole congregation might be visited with abounding leisure every month. Every family in his Church would probably be heard of by him in some way every week. His grand difficulty is want of work—and he is rusting out from having no adequate employment. And yet with every thing wasting and dying around him, this very man lamented that he had no

field for his powers, and that the openings for
the ministry were most inequitably distributed.
The skipper of a schooner on which every rope
was sagging, and her very masts reeling from
his own lethargy and negligence, complaining,
as he lay smoking on the cluttered deck, that
great injustice had been done him in not making him the commander of a seventy-four!
Surely the apostle well says, that those who
"purchase for themselves a good degree and
great boldness in the faith which is in Christ
Jesus," are they who "have used the office of
a minister well." What possible hindrance is
there in any moderate Church to the minister
taking the personal charge and superintendence
of the Sunday-school of his own Church? I
say "moderate Church," but I might justly
say any Church, for I am persuaded it is a perfectly feasible and a most appropriate work for
every pastor in every Church. Such an arrangement brings the whole subject and interest of Sunday-school instruction under his own
eye, enables him to see how far the important
work is adequately done, gives him the oppor-

17*

tunity of a personal direction and control of the operation, and of a fair and easy correction of the errors and mistakes perceived. It makes him alive to the vast influence and interests of the scheme ; awakens his own heart more and more to the cultivation of personal, practical religion among the young ; gives him a deeper interest in their welfare and happiness ; and prepares him for more minute and enlarged influence in his own relation to them, and to the families to which they belong. It inspires the teachers with new zeal and love in their work —awakens a lasting personal affection and confidence toward himself—unites them about him as a body of friends beloved, and gives energy and spirit to the operation as it proceeds. It brings him into immediate personal connection with the children of his flock—makes him a helper of their joy, and a partner of their welfare—opens their hearts to his ministry, and attracts them to himself. It establishes unquestioned authority in the school, secures its order, and gives a new reverence from teachers and children to the superintendent's place and position. It imparts a practical and effective character to the minister's own work, gives him more and more an adaptation to the business of his ministry, and makes him more efficient and real in every other department of his duty. It is the very manufacture which the raw material of a multitude of ministers requires to transform them into useful, appropriate, and practical agents in the Lord's house. It mortalizes their ministry, by bringing them down to a practical shape and compelling the cultivation of a common-sense habit of teaching and address. It converts their abstractions into realities, and by making them the " teachers of babes " makes them the more intelligible and useful teachers for all. " When will ministers cease to try to feed their sheep out of horse-racks ?" said a plain man once to me, in expressing his dissatisfaction with a sermon which he could not understand. Well, when will they ? Never, I think, until they fulfill the second neglected command, "Feed my lambs." In no way will a pastor become more alive to the real necessities and condition of his flock, than in this personal devotion to the ministry of the children's church. It puts him into immediate and easy communication with them all. It enables him to reach the affections and sympathies of the adults, through these happiest and most accessible channels. It thus binds the whole flock together, and produces and maintains abiding harmony and mutual affection among all. And whether I consider the effects upon the school, upon the teachers, upon the children, upon the families, upon the congregation, or upon himself, I must say that no employment in the ministry appears to me more real in spirit, more promising in character, or richer in results, than this personal engagement of the pastor as the actual head of his Sunday-school. What rich blessings flow from it upon all, none but they who have most thoroughly tried it can really tell. And I am sure that no minister who really loves his Master's work, and wishes to follow his Master's pattern, will voluntarily sacrifice the reciprocated blessings thus presented, when he has once made a fair experiment of **the**

work.   Thus will the pastor share the reality
of his interest in this blessed effort, and awake
to the importance of extending it as widely
and as efficiently as possible in the world
abroad.

XXI.

 HAVE earnestly advocated the assumption by the pastor of the superintendence of his own Church school. I believe this to be for himself, for the school, for the children, and for the Church, in all respects, the best plan. I deem it in reality one of the most important parts of his whole work in the ministry. The pastor who can be the most successful instrument of guiding and blessing the children of his flock, in the ways of religion and truth, will be in the highest degree and scale a permanent blessing to the Church and the world. And as the Sunday-school has been so clearly displayed as the Church for children, the adapted and appropriate instrument of teach-

ing and blessing for them—the most intimate, intelligent, and authoritative relation in which the minister can stand to this, is the most desirable and important for himself as for them. In our smaller Churches, whether in town or country, there can be no difficulty in carrying out this plan completely. And abounding blessings would flow from it, on every side, to all concerned. In our larger Churches I am aware that many ministers imagine it a labor beyond their power or strength. In some cases it may be so. I should be most unwilling to urge unnecessary or impossible burdens upon the ministry. Their toils and duties, if adequately carried out, are abundant, and often overwhelming. But I would suggest, could not a wiser husbandry of time and a more methodical arrangement of labor, gain for them the strength and opportunity which such a work as this requires? If not, is not the work itself so important and desirable that some other occupation less directly bearing upon the welfare of redeemed souls might be yielded for the sake of it? Far from being

an excessive fatigue, it would be found a re-
freshment and an encouraging aid for the public services of the Sabbath's worship. The
more cordially and faithfully it shall be carried
out, the more deeply will a faithful minister
find himself interested and engaged in it. It
will come to be in his view one of the most
desirable, as well as one of the most effective
parts of his ministry. And it can by no
means be considered irrelevant or unrequired,
for one who is to give himself wholly to the
work of the ministry—to continue in its labors
—to be as a gentle nurse among the children
of his flock, and so affectionately desirous of
them that he is willing to impart unto them,
not the Gospel of God only, but also his own
life, because they are dear unto him. The
more an earnest pastor labors in this work,
only the more will he desire to spend and be
spent therein, that by all means he may save
some.

But it is also objected, that certain ministers
have no adaptation of taste or character for
such a work as this. I can only say, if they

have no love for children, and no desire especially to bless them, they are manifestly wanting in a most important characteristic of the
Saviour's example, and an indispensable qualification for a useful and successful ministry.
If it is a fault of the heart, or of the deliberate
judgment, in this relation, they must forfeit a
precious field and department of usefulness,
and render reasonably doubtful their usefulness in any other field of pastoral duty. If it
be a defect of habit and education, the very
practice is to teach them a more important lesson in the ministry than they have yet learned.
Nothing appears more offensive to intelligent
and reasonable men than an affectation of
peculiar learning, in the employment of high-
sounding words or far-reaching allusions in the
ministry of the Gospel. The New Testament
seems to say to ministers, on every page, in
the words and examples of its great Founder
and His apostles, " Be simple." Our own in-
comparable translation has transferred this
very simplicity of utterance for the common
use of the poor and the ignorant. And the

18

minister who wishes to be wiser and grander than the New Testament, will find himself just so much less acceptable to the most intelligent portion of his flock. The relations of his ministry to the children will be the very lesson which he needs. And the habit of dealing with them, and providing for them, and watching over them, will furnish the very supply of feeling, power, and adaptation in which such a man finds himself to be deficient. His heart, his mind, and his habits will all grow rapidly and healthfully under such an exercise and employment as the Sunday-school gives him, for greater and more permanent usefulness in other departments of his duty as well as in this. Unity and harmony will reign under his administration in this work. The Sunday-school teachers will welcome him, and labor with him with delight. They will combine to reverence his character, to repose upon his sincerity, to delight in their relations to him, and to be his chosen, earnest, and faithful friends. The reciprocal effect upon the ministry and the school will be equally valuable. And the whole garden of the Lord which he has been set to cultivate will revive and flourish under this extending and practical influence of his personal labors in every department of his divinely appointed work.

If, after all, the minister really can not undertake the actual charge and superintendence of the Sunday-school, can he not habitually visit it, and become personally acquainted with its operations and its needs? What shall hinder his giving an hour of every Sabbath to a personal observation of the work? Let him thus oversee the superintendence of another, and become personally familiar with the teachers and the details of the operation, as they are managed in his sight. He will thus become acquainted with the several ability and adaptation of the teachers. He will see who are really useful in their work, and likely to be his effective adjuncts in ministering the Gospel to the youth of his flock. He will be able to advise the superintendent in reference to many important facts and methods of usefulness, as they arise before him. For what is the whole school but a part of his responsibility in the ministry? And what are superintendents and teachers, but parts of his ministry, severally carrying out his work, and helpers of his joy ? This regular Sabbath visitation will be an eminent blessing to the school and to himself. He will learn much, and he will be able to teach much in the practical efficiency of his ministry from this habit, which can be acquired nowhere else. To neglect this is mere negligence of duty. The minister may as well say he has no time to preach, or visit the suffering and the sick, the fatherless and the widows in their affliction. For what has he been sent into the world, and raised up in the Church, and received the Lord's commission, and assumed the care and teaching of those for whom the Saviour died ? How can any part of the work of the Gospel flourish under the labors of a man so heartless, so indifferent, so indolent, or so secularized in mind and spirit ?

Can not the minister give the teachers of his Sunday-school a weekly instruction upon the subject of their teaching ? Let it be a lecture, or a Bible-class, or a teachers' meeting, in whatever way organized and arranged. Some special hour devoted to their work he can surely give. And he surely ought to give it. Has he no adaptation or acquirement for this either ? What can he do that more truly belongs to his pastoral office ? At any rate, he is supposed to have studied the Scriptures more thoroughly than the youthful and busy teachers who are gathered around him. If not, then it will be a blessed employment for him to meet and study an hour a week with them. Thus they may grow together in a knowledge of that word of inspiration which is able to make them wise unto salvation, through faith in Christ Jesus.

Can not the pastor habitually or occasionally preach the Gospel especially and personally to the young ? How much of public preaching is utterly unintelligible and useless to them ? Often, necessarily, of subjects beyond their reach. Often, unnecessarily, in language which they can not comprehend. If this must be so, in much of the public teaching of the pulpit, can there not be special teaching adapted to their capacities and wants? There is here no additional labor imposed, no excessive demand made upon time too occupied, or energies too much taxed, or minds too full of other duties. If every pastor would give one sermon on every Sunday, especially addressed to the young, and designed and prepared to teach them, he would find himself enlarging his direct usefulness in this particular work, and equally advancing the value and benefit of every other class of his public and private labors in religious instruction also. The parents and adults of his flock will learn as much; and love as much the teaching for themselves, when he speaks to the youth directly and simply, as when he addresses them in a deeper and more mature discourse.

I hope I shall not be censured as having said too much upon this special branch of the subject before us. I can not understand how any Christian minister can feel himself excused from a personal, practical consideration of this great part of his appointed work. Whatever is to be given up, the pastor who follows in the steps of his Master must not give up the children. The Sunday-school everywhere feels the want of the mind of the ministry in its welfare—a real pastoral devotion to its success. The pastor must be its living, actual head. It should constantly receive the stimulus and encouragement of his presence and his example. He should have the sweet solace of the children's relation to him, a comfort to his wearied spirit. The minister deprived of this loses one of the most precious of the pleasures of his work. And I can not but earnestly entreat the affectionate and serious contemplation of my brethren in the ministry to the whole subject in its relations to themselves, which I have attempted to suggest.

XXII

THE duties of the Church to the Sunday-school will necessarily suggest the resulting consideration of the reciprocal duties of the Sunday-school to the Church. Let us not forget that on each side they are both but secondary instruments, and the real duty of both is to the Great Head and Lord of the Church. From love and faithfulness to Christ, the Church is to be loving and faithful to the lambs of the flock, and maintain and extend the Sunday-school in all its interests and claims for their benefit. And from the same love and faithfulness to Christ the Saviour of the whole body, are the teachers of the Sunday-school to be faithful to the Church of God, whose members and agents they are in the Lord's work. They are employed for the special and very important work of educating the children of the Church for its service and privileges, that in them, as a seed to serve Him, the Lord Jesus may be glorified in His Church. In this relation there must be, as an indispensable purpose in the Sunday-school, the cultivation of a spirit of peaceful and affectionate fellowship with the Church to which the school belongs, and a just submission to its higher authority and welfare. A narrow, sectarian temper in any Christian, I trust I shall be the last to inculcate upon any. But we can not take any other ground, with a good conscience, than that our several Church connections are the subject of providence in God, and of reasonable and adequate choice and determination in ourselves. In giving a reason for the hope that is in us, we ought not to hide the facts that we are where we are in the household of faith, for sufficient cause, and with sincere affection. Whatever our Church may be, we have an allegiance to it, and must maintain a due regard to its authority, and a proper consideration for its welfare and success. The Sunday-school must always consider itself a part of the Church, and cultivate a relation of harmony and submission in this connection. Any starting of an independent authority, or setting up of a new republic in its management, will not only be most unseemly, and out of due order, but in most cases counteract much of the good which the school is likely to accomplish. The pastor's presence, guidance, and control must be always welcomed. The manifest plan must include him, and demand him ; and if he be unfaithful or negligent in this precious field of his privilege and responsibility, he must not be permitted to offer as an excuse the assumed or practical independence of the school of his authority and influence. I have been amazed to find how often and how unreasonably such jealousies have arisen among the ministry. I have seen some instances of very childish and absurd sensitiveness upon this point in ministers, who should have felt themselves quite superior to such a thought. And yet I have also seen

schools and teachers far from faultless in this
relation, claiming for themselves an independent authority and right of direction, and even
foolishly refusing and withstanding the affectionate and fraternal approach of a pastor in
his desire to assist and encourage them. It is
vain to expect the dews of heaven in an atmosphere like this. The ministry of the Gospel
must be regarded and acknowledged as set up
for the teaching of the Church of God. And
all the agencies and instruments of religious
teaching in the Church must be considered as
part of their work, and as directly responsible
to them, in whom this whole responsibility of
teaching is placed. So far as schools are connected with Churches, there can be no doubt
upon this subject. And even in schools which
are established on an independent foundation
in the necessity of their origin, we have already
seen, there will arise a Church connection and
a ministry which will soon settle the position
here also.

That much depends upon a loving and harmonious spirit in our Sunday-school labors for

their success and happiness, it would be vain
to deny. Let teachers, above all things, avoid
a separatist and self-exalting spirit, and try to
feel that not he who commendeth himself is
approved in this respect, but he whom the
Lord commendeth. Let children be brought
up as parts of the household of the faith—not
indifferent to their Church relations—and by
no means taught that it is of no consequence
where they belong and to whom they belong,
or where their Sabbath worship may be employed, so that they are really and truly in
heart belonging to the Lord. The cultivation
of each individual estate thoroughly and well,
is the best cultivation for the highest prosperity of the whole country in which they all are.
And the faithful care and watchfulness in
every Church over all its collective interests
and welfare, is, beyond all question, the wisest
and happiest way to promote the universal
welfare and happiness of the Lord's cause on
the earth. I feel this of special value and
truth in our Sunday-schools. It is a secondary fact in importance, but far from an unim-

portant one, to attach children in their affections and habits to the Church of their inherit-
ance. The tendrils of youthful religion must
clasp a near and adequate support. Their
early piety demands the aid and nursing of
the outward connection. And I should far
rather see them trained in their attachment
to a body much less desirable in my view, than
brought up in the more general ignorance and
skepticism of the value of Church relations,
and left to be driven by the wild winds of future controversy, to attach themselves, or to
become attached, as may happen, to whatever
shall be most convenient, or run the more
likely hazard of living and dying loose from all.
True Christian liberty allows every one to be
fully persuaded in his own mind. But then
it *does* allow him to be *fully* persuaded. And
no process is more likely to be successful, and
no sight is more beautiful, than to see the
youth of a flock trained in happy regularity
and devotion in the worship and principles,
and affectionate maintenance of the Church to
which they belong. Vain and most unprofit-

able is the Neapolitan plan of promiscuous dwelling in the streets. Let us maintain and carry out the simple Protestant Christian scheme of loving all who love the Lord Jesus Christ in sincerity, but walking ourselves by the rule which we have attained, and minding the thing which we have been taught. This, I think, the Sunday-school of every Church should distinctly regard. And, therefore, I urge, as a first principle of reciprocal obligation, this cultivation of a conscious and acknowledged union with the Church on which it lives and from which it grows.

I should be sorry to be considered as giving this subject undue consequence. But I esteem its practical influence very valuable. That our little ones shall grow up in affectionate relations with all these outward facts and agencies of their enjoyment of Gospel teaching, I have already spoken of as among the important, actual advantages of our whole scheme. And to me, certainly, one of the highest pleasures of my life is to see generations of youth growing up around me, who learned to love

me and my ministry in their infancy, and ad-
here to me and encompass me as faithful ad-
juvants in their early maturity and age.
Pleasant as are all additions to the Lord's
table among us, I should be obliged to confess
that none seem so pleasant as those of the
children who have grown up with me, and
seem thus to be the fruits of my past toils,
and tenderness, and prayer. Beautiful are the
blossoms and fruit beheld growing in every or-
chard. But it is not in man, and it ought not
to be, not to rejoice with peculiar joy in the
special fruitfulness of trees which his own hand
has planted and tended, and the oncoming of
which his grateful and hopeful eye has watched
with delight in all the years of their advancement. I can not but say it is far from indifferent to me that my Sunday-school children
should be Episcopalians, and continue and
grow as members of St. George's Church, and
that I should still find them bringing forth
fruit in my age. Accordingly, while there is
the common, all-important Gospel teaching
for all, there may be, with great propriety, the

additional, distinctive, positive teaching for each, of attachment to their own Church and school. Adams of Wintringham, when reproached by his neighbors that his church was filled by drawing off from them, simply replied, "Salt your sheep, brethren, and they will not stray." Thus are our Sunday-schools to minister to our flocks by furnishing attractions as well as instructions to our lambs. They are the nursery of the family, and are to make their little charge happy in their home, loving their home, and grateful to abide at home. In this way the Sunday-school becomes an important aid to the Church in the individual connection, and equally so in the extending of the great cause. Our youth grow up with a Church spirit as well as a Christian spirit. The future Churches of the nation rise up in an intelligent and consolidated power. The various portions of the Lord's house grow and flourish under the influence and agency of this whole work, and successive generations show the importance and value of the influence in the strength and vigor of the result perpetu-

ated. The Church reaps the blessing from
the school in the enlarged and generous action,
as well as in the intelligent and affectionate
support of its members thus taught. And in
the true and abiding prosperity of the Churches
of the Lord, the Lord Jesus, the Head of the
whole Church, is Himself glorified and honored. I had not thought to have said so much
of this point when I began ; but it has grown
upon my hands as I have written, I hope not
unreasonably, and postpones some other lines
of thought to my next.

19*

XXIII.

HOPE you will not think I have insisted too much on Church relations. I am sometimes disposed to fear that in our union efforts to spread the Gospel in which my heart truly delights, we may overlook the propriety and importance of maintaining in their due order our various Church lines, and lose our family obligations, interests, and pleasures, in the more general efforts of social advancement or national patriotism. And yet we are by no means without dangers of sectarism on the other side, and must therefore strive to give to each their due and proportionate consideration, and try to love our Church and teach our children to love it, without teaching them or allowing them to love any other Christians less. In this special

connection comes the subject of Church catechisms as a Sunday-school exercise. We can
not well avoid its consideration. In this I
should again say, the Bible is our great book
for Sunday-school instruction. Yet every class
of Christians have organized and arranged their
peculiar interpretations of Scripture teaching
in catechisms, as compendiums of the Christian
doctrines which are deemed by them of special
importance. In some Sunday-schools the
whole body of instruction is given in these selected catechisms. In others, perhaps, they
may be entirely neglected. It is evident, however, that two different rules must be laid
down here in application to schools which belong to particular Churches, and schools which
are gathered and taught independently of all
Church relations. In the latter, of which
there are many, surely no catechism can be
properly taught, unless it shall be some Scripture catechism which includes merely the great
evangelical doctrines and duties, in which the
Scripture instruction is perfectly plain, and re-
garding which there can be no reasonable dis-

pute. In the former, or Church-schools, it is equally clear that there may be a propriety and a reasonable obligation to give a fair consideration to the authorized and adopted catechism of the Church. While, therefore, I am content to yield a certain attention to these catechisms, I can never exalt them out of a merely subordinate place. In practical use, they are dull, unintelligible, and unattractive to children, and it is always a burden on the minds of children to learn them, and a very dry and heavy work for teachers to teach or to expound them. I can never speak of them as in themselves desirable. I have great doubts how far they are especially positively useful. I have no doubt that actual, simple Scriptural instruction is far more so. And though I must yield the point of subordinate uniformity to Church appointment, in this reciprocal Church relation, in Sunday-schools which belong to particular Churches, and acknowledge a secondary influence of these formularies in giving particular shapes of religious instruction as thus required ; I confess I write and speak

even so much as this under the constraint of
the idea of abstract obligation, and not as the
spontaneous language of my own experience.
Though I have taken a small portion of the
time, on one morning out of four, to teach and
expound our Episcopal Church catechism, as,
were I a Presbyterian minister, I should have
done the Assembly's catechism, I can not recall the avowals of opinion which I made some
years since in Brooklyn at the New York State
Convention of Sunday-school teachers, or ad-
mit that any further experience has led me to
change them. Then I said, " The great business of a Sunday-school teacher is conversion,
not catechisms, not confessions of faith. Our
schools are to be Bible-schools, technically and
entirely. A man may teach a child to repeat
the catechism ten years over successively, and
yet that child gain no spiritual idea. But no
Christian man can take the 15th chapter of St.
Luke and teach it to a little child, or to a family of children, without imparting influence
that must and will produce its effect. I have
no sympathy with that miserable scheme which

would take away from you all that is vital and glorious in your work, and persuade you to be the mere agent of sectarian teaching. I will agree that when minds are better trained, and hearts are early drawn to the Saviour, cate- chisms and confessions may then be useful and instructive ; but God has never promised con- version to the Confession of Faith, or to the Thirty-nine Articles, or to the Westminister Catechism ; nor can you find the word in the Bible, 'Go teach the catechism, and whosever learneth it shall be saved.' The simple prin- ciple of the Bible is to teach the Bible. I have no disposition to shrink from the responsibility of every part of it. There is not a history which does not exhibit some spiritual truth, able to make wise unto salvation, through faith in Christ Jesus. There is not a single narrative or fact which in the hands of a spir- itually-minded teacher will not be brought out as a definite instrumentality for the instruction and, if God shall please, the conversion of the soul.".

These were words freely spoken in an im-

promptu address. But the principle involved
in them abides with me, confirmed and
strengthened by continued and enlarged experience. From a child are our children to know
the Holy Scriptures, which are given by inspiration of God, and are profitable for them as
for others, for doctrine, for reproof, for correction, for instruction in righteousness. This
wonderful book is always interesting, attractive, and instructive. No children in our
schools are too young to delight in its stories,
or to comprehend the history and the love of
that great Saviour in whom all its instructions
meet. It never wearies their attention, or fails
to awaken their conversation and their thoughts.
Its language is the most intelligible, its narra-
tions are the most simple and natural, its principles and truths are the most clear and easily
comprehended, which can be given to the
young. And the time expended in its study
and its exposition in a well-ordered Sunday-
school, is always found too short and too rapid
for the great purpose to which it is devoted.
The late Dr. James Alexander says, in his let-

ters to the editor of a Sunday-school journal, with equal truth and beauty, " Let me beg of you to take it as a prominent, perpetual object of selections for your journal, to hold up the great truth that the Bible is the book to educate the age.   Why not have it the chief thing in the family, in the school, in the academy, in the university ?   The day is coming ; and if you and I can introduce the minutest corner of this wedge, we shall be benefactors of the race.   I can amuse a child about the Bible.   I can teach logic, rhetoric, ethics, and salvation from the Bible.   May we not have a Bible-school ?   Sow the seed, my dear friend, meekly, prayerfully ; it must grow.   The Bible, the Bible, it is this which must save America.   It is this which must save the Church, not by spasmodic transitory attempts on emergencies, but by being a perennial well of divine truth.   Don't try to vary the Bible language too much ; say what you will, it is most intelligible to children.   Don't try too much to improve upon the Bible.   Let what you add be explanatory and brief.   You will readily see how my thoughts course one another in the channel which but for Sunday-schools would never have existed for me. I more and more sicken at human dilutions of the Word, and love the taste of the fresh fountain." What could be more appropriate than these expressions of that beloved and excellent man in the connection in which we now place them?

The book for the Sunday-schol is the Bible. Every portion of its history and its teaching should come up for study in its turn. Its various parts must be made to illustrate and confirm each other. Children must be familiarized with its use, and accustomed to refer to its various parts easily and freely. And even when catechisms are taught, the proofs and authorities should always be found and stated from the Scriptures themselves. Accordingly, the very first demand of a Sabbath-school teacher is to be personally an assiduous reader of the Bible, and familiar with its language and contents. The general structure of its books—the succession of their contents—the special subjects particularly taught in each—the location of particular facts and stories—must all be made familiar to a teacher's mind by the habit of constant and attentive personal reading. The Church commits this Bible teaching of the young to Sunday-school teachers. The pastor watches over it, assists it, expounds it, prepares for it. The teachers owe it as a reciprocal obligation to the Church to be qualified by familiar knowledge of the sacred book, to instruct with faithfulness and ease. This requires only a constant, earnest reading, with a desire and purpose to retain and understand. Some of our poorest Christians are often found mighty in the Scriptures. It has been often a great delight to me to meet the instances in proof of this. It does not demand peculiar talent or higher education. It requires only a love and knowledge of the Bible itself, a knowledge within the reach of the most burdened and laborious Christians in their earthly affairs, if a love of the Word be in the heart. And we may well ask Sunday-school teachers, How frequently do you read the Bible through ? How often have you ever read it

through ?   How much do you really study it
as a whole, with the desire and purpose to understand it?   This is fundamental in your
work.   It is endless as your privilege.   If you
really love it you will continue to study it only
with increasing advantage and delight, and
find no end thereof.

XXIV.

THE Bible being our one book of habitual Sunday-school teaching, it is a very important and interesting question, how we are to teach it with effect. There is a skill to be acquired and employed in the use of this divine instrument, the value of which is far beyond all the labor and thought which its acquisition will demand. The teacher must "remember that although the conversion of his scholars can be accomplished by divine agency alone, it is for him to win their affections, captivate their tastes, improve their minds, convince their judgments, and impress their consciences. This is his work, and for its right performance he is responsible. With a deep sense of that responsibility, let him diligently employ every means to qualify himself for his momentous duties. To earnest prayer let him unite earnest labor, deeming no task too arduous, and no sacrifice too great to secure for each of his youthful charge an interest in the great salvation, and a place among the people of God."* Thus to teach the sacred Scriptures to advantage and with success must require much thought and preparation.

The particular lesson must be previously studied with diligence and care. I have spoken enough of the general study of the Bible necessary as an habitual employment. This can not be relied upon as adequate for a particular lesson. None but those whose minds are fully devoted to Scriptural study, and in whom the engrafted Word is dwelling richly with all wisdom, can be qualified to take up a particular lesson and teach it with any effect. And they are habitually the very persons who will be least inclined to trust

* Groser's Illustrative Teaching. Randolph, New York.

themselves to any such general preparation. The particular lesson must be studied for the special occasion with all the means of assistance within the reach of the teacher. A good practical commentary, like Scott or Henry, is an important guide. The parallel references in Scott are an invaluable aid. Whatever can be brought to bear upon the selected passage for instruction becomes valuable in its degree. But the time and thought during the week must be conscientiously given to the study, and to the study of this particular passage. It is an unspeakable benefit for the teacher to gain a full and thorough understanding of even one selected passage of Scripture in the week. Questions of every kind should be proposed to himself, for his own consideration and reply. The subjects which the passage contains should be brought forth in distinct points. Notes should be made as extensively as possible for the exposition of the portion in actual teaching. The mind and thought should be given to it, as a subject for personal consideration maturely and frequently. The habit of this will enlarge the mind of the teacher, and act as really and as effectually on his own attainments from the Scriptures as on the instructions which he gives. I must consider this study indispensable ; indispensable to usefulness to others—indispensable for personal satisfaction in the work. An hour on Saturday evening, or a hurried glance over the questions appointed, is perfectly insufficient. And the want of this conscientious, earnest study is one grand reason of the want of interest in many classes, and the want of success in many teachers.

The habit of daily, constant prayer in this connection must be maintained. It must be prayer for divine teaching. The humble, praying mind will be remarkably guided and taught in the study of the Scriptures. God has promised, and will never withhold, His Spirit and His wisdom from those who ask Him. The very habit of prayer gives utterance to the mouth for God. It domesticates the mind in the Word of God. It familiarizes the thoughts and affections with its contemplation. And often more effectually than all commentaries, will sincere prayer for guidance open the path, and clear up the difficulties perceived. It must be special prayer for the children taught. The names of children must be habitually remembered and mentioned in prayer with special petitions for the peculiar blessings and mercies needed in their family relations, or their personal temptations and dangers. How much a teacher may in this way be made a blessing to the souls of children, none can tell. His private, secret prayers may bring salvation upon the house in which no common, and perhaps no secret prayer, is offered. We little remember the one all-applying text, "Ye have not because ye ask not." Let a teacher think of this. Have I really asked? How often? For what? With what perseverance? It is a most precious part of a teacher's privilege and office to be a living and effective intercessor for his little flock. And the richest blessings may descend upon them, carrying down an influence to other generations, and into an eternal world, through his private, secret supplications. But such prayer must not be confined to a particular class. The whole body of teachers should feel themselves partners in prayer for the whole school in which they are engaged. The circle of private prayer should surround the whole, and each should become the habitual intercessor for all. Thus divine mercies will descend upon all, and God will pour out His blessings upon all, while the united prayer shall return into the bosom of each.

In the actual, practical teaching of a Bible lesson thus prepared by study and prayer, there is required peculiar tact and skill. Children are easily interested, but volatile in attention, and superficial in thought. And, therefore, their attention is not only to be secured by instructing address—but maintained by variety of teaching. Mere didactic, abstract instruction will not meet their wants. Still less a barren answer derived from them to particular questions prepared. The object is to interest their thoughts—to teach them

and help them to think—to fasten the subject of teaching upon their memory—and to
give them some instruction which shall be permanent and effectual.　This is only to be done
by a system of illustration, from every variety
of source accessible to the teacher, and adapted
to the minds of children.　The whole system
of divine teaching in the Scripture is of this
description.　An endless variety of story and
biography and comparison is employed there to
make every truth more clear and manifest in
its personal application to those for whom they
are all proclaimed.　And the preacher or
teacher most of all confined to the mere Bible
without note or comment for study, will habitually become in the very pattern of the Bible,
the most disposed and ready to illustrate its
truths by comparisons and facts bearing them
out.　An anecdote read, or a fact witnessed,
really carrying out the particular point of
teaching in the lesson, is always effectual and
impressive.　These facts should bear upon the
point directly, and not merely be a story told
—still less, as I have sometimes seen, a book

read by the teacher to the class, as a reward for
going through the lesson prescribed.   The illustration should be short and applicable immediately, so that the child shall discern its propriety and force.   Thus the Saviour taught.
The lilies of the field—the fowls of the air—
the fish in the net—the falling tower of Siloam
—the cruelty of Pilate, and a multitude of
such facts, constantly seen and easily understood, were habitually employed by Him to
enforce and explain the truths which He would
teach.   The prophets and apostles taught upon
the same plan, under the same divine teaching
of the Spirit.   This it is which has made the
Bible the book of deepest and most abiding
interest, as well as the most easily intelligible
to the youthful and the poor of every age.
The Sunday-school teacher must adopt this
model, and carry it out as faithfully and effectually as he can.

The lesson must be taught in the plainest
and simplest language.   Often the very words
will be found unintelligible to the children.
I once asked a class of intelligent little boys

in a lesson on the second chapter of Ruth, the meaning of "gleaning"—and not one could tell me. It was a term out of their habit of use, and required explanation from other habits than they had ever seen. Such instances will often occur. The teacher can not be too simple in instruction. It is a very high as well as valuable attainment to be able to do this. To do it effectually demands a variety of information—habitual patience and self-control—and a thorough knowledge of the real worth and meaning of words. Let a teacher take nothing for granted in the knowledge of children— but bring out the amount of their information, and the readiness of their thought, by constant and simple questions addressed thus to each. To use simple words is a most important requisite for deep and real teaching. All extraneous conversation must be cut off, and the attention kept fixed on the one subject, which is the appointed subject of study. Step after step must they go forward in the lesson—with the effort and purpose that it shall be thoroughly understood. An hour will soon pass in the effort to make ten verses of Scripture plain to a class of little ones.   And the more they understand and are interested in it, only the more difficult will it become to restrain the association of their thoughts, and to confine them to the actual line of teaching in hand.

XXV.

HAT is more interesting than to see a Sunday-school teacher effectively operating upon the scheme which I have described—a class of boys or girls, intently listening, deeply interested, and affectionately devoted to their teacher—turning over their Bibles for references—eagerly answering the questions proposed, or as eagerly proposing their questions in return? I have watched the operation of such a work for the Lord until my whole attention has become absorbed in the one class, and I felt my eyes glistening with tears of delight. For such a work there will be required, beyond the information and simplicity of teaching of which I have spoken, great tenderness of manner, real affection of heart, manifest love for the souls of the children, and for the Saviour to whom they are directed. The work must be all sincere, real, and fully confident in the success and blessing which are desired. The teacher must feel that the benefit to be derived is mutual, and while he is refreshing and guiding others, he is also refreshed and guided himself. Hopefulness in his undertaking is of inestimable value to him. His own cheerful and confiding manner will be imparted to his children. They will partake of his spirit and reflect back upon him the exciting and encouraging influence which they receive. Thus the whole engagement becomes a pleasure of the highest kind to both, and a source of advantage and profit to all.

We will suppose the teacher seated before his class in this cheerful, hopeful spirit. They welcome him on the Sabbath morning as one of their chief and chosen friends. They rejoice to see him, and to unite with him in the work at hand. Deep seriousness as well as joy and delight mark their union in the religious exercises which open the school. As each child is a unit before the teacher, so is the spirit and aspect of the whole class a unit before the superintendent. There is perfect drill in quietness and attention among them all. They thus minister exceedingly to the pleasure and prosperity of the whole assembly. The opening worship ended, no time is lost or wasted in talking or idleness. Instantly every one has his Bible, and every Bible is opened at the appointed place. They begin at once to read the lesson through—by single verses around the class. The teacher in a few words opens the subject which the lesson contains, and lays before them the story, or the fact, or the doctrine, which they are to consider. Every thing then opens in a ready and regular way, and all are prepared to enter upon the work before them with delight. Then come the questions upon each succeeding verse, in which the object is not so much to get direct answers to simple questions as to engage the minds of the children to think upon the subject proposed, and to fasten these thoughts in their minds and memory. Accordingly, every general question is broken up by particular questions, illustrating the point which it presents ; and every answer suggests new questions, making clear and certain the information which the answer presents. On every verse or every question some extraneous illustration will occur to mind, or has been already prepared by the teacher— some anecdote, some fact from history, from natural history, or from personal events, to make the whole point more vivid and distinct. Such illustrations should be short, and not run out into long stories. They should be immediately apposite and apparent, that the minds of children may see the resemblance or analogy at once. They should be very simple, so that the illustration shall not need more explanation than the lesson which it proposes to explain. They must be presented in a concise and distinct form, and not dragged on in a sleepy, heavy way. Every such illustration well directed will awaken a new train of thought in the youthful mind, and stir them up to new life in the subject before them. There must be care, therefore, that the whole train is not led

off upon a new branch, a mere diversion. The
constant connection must be maintained with
the lesson in hand, and every part of the instruction must run directly in that one line,
while the whole must be guided to a personal,
religious application to the hearts of the children. Thus the work goes on in increasing interest for all, as the time goes by. And the
whole time seems too short for the engagement
they have had, and full of interest and delight
to them in it. The closing exercises of praise
and prayer are but a more solemn illustration
of the united, affectionate attention than the
opening. And the school closes, with the universal feeling of delight in the minds of teacher
and children.

If this description could be carried out
through a whole school, no employment could
be more delightful, and perhaps no religious
agency or instrument more effectual. It would
be the Sunday-school enterprise in its perfec-
tion of operation and result. We may hardly
anticipate this. But we may certainly work
toward it; and encourage each other to attain

it, in a constantly increasing measure of success. In such an operation, the minds and hearts of children become intensely interested in the employment—many are brought up to a full and decided profession and maintenance of their love and obedience to a Saviour, in all His appointed ordinances, and in the whole duties of a Christian life. It is a work of real salvation, and of abounding blessing. · As our schools go on, the number of faithful, useful teachers constantly increases. Every year gives us manifest improvement in our style of work, and equally manifest advance in the results we attain. And the longer we are occupied, and the more enlarged becomes our experience in this blessed enterprise, the more satisfactory and compensating it appears. Thousands of children have gained salvation here. They are growing up to that "great multitude which no man can number, of all nations, and kindreds, and peoples, and tongues, standing before the throne, and before the Lamb, clothed with white robes, and with palms in their hands, crying with a loud voice, Salvation to

our God which sitteth upon the throne, and
unto the Lamb." The living Church of God
" clothes herself with them all, as with an or-
nament, and binds them on her as a bride
doeth." Hundreds of teachers are receiving
the glorious promise of the Lord by His an-
gel, "They that be 'teachers' [margin] shall
shine as the brightness of the firmament—and
they that turn many to righteousness, as the
stars for ever and ever." What glory already
fills the heavenly courts from this work of
heaven on the earth ! What encouragement
abounds in it still upon the earth ! As generations go on, in the advancing progress of the
Lord's redeemed, new blessings and new instruments of blessing arise to us here. And every
year enlarges our hopes and establishes our
convictions in the worth of this enterprise for
the Lord, in which we are occupied for His
glory, and for the everlasting welfare of the
children He hath purchased with His own
precious blood.

I can only say to my beloved fellow-teachers
in closing this series of familiar letters, ad-

dressed personally to one of their number, but intended for the encouragement of them all, Let us work for the Lord, with a ready mind and an earnest will. Do it as His work, and do it for Him. He will increase His gifts of grace and glory upon us—in our own experience and enjoyment—and He will cause His blessed work to prosper in our hands. He gives us, as our reward, the love of our children—the gratitude of their parents—the approval of His Church—the sweeter peace of our own possession of His Spirit—the pleasure of the toil—the actual growth of our own souls in grace by it—the salvation of the precious souls committed to us—the promotion of the Saviour's glory here—the welcome of the Saviour's smile and approbation hereafter—a name of usefulness in His family below—a name of honor in His family above. We can not be without our reward—abounding rewards. Let us be simple in motive, sincere in spirit, faithful in duty, persevering in hope—sowing our precious seed in the morning; in the evening, withholding not our hands, but sowing still with unrelaxing zeal, and in due time we shall reap, if we faint not. A commander of a British vessel of war, sailing from the Cape of Good Hope, was charged with the convoy of a little sloop of value, to England. They were in mutual sight for many days. But a storm arose, and separated them finally. The armed vessel pursued her course homeward, the captain not expecting to see his little charge again. He entered the channel and anchored off Portsmouth in a fog, with a heavy heart, in remembrance of her. But when the thick fog lifted, what was his surprise at seeing the little lost craft anchored in peace directly by his side. In equal ignorance of his course, her commander had dropped his anchor there. Ah, what a joyful meeting there will be with many of our little ones, too, when, safe at last, we see them there. Doubt, perhaps despair, for them may have possessed us long. Ignorance of them may have distressed us much. But when the darkness has passed, and the true light shineth, we shall welcome them with delight, and rejoice over them with singing.

But which shall prosper, whether this or that, let us never forget that our Blessed Master says to each of us, " BE THOU FAITHFUL UNTO DEATH, AND I WILL GIVE THEE A CROWN OF LIFE."

THE END.